SWIMMING
into
DARKNESS

SWIMMING
into
DARKNESS

Gail HELGASON

COTEAU BOOKS
WWW.COTEAUBOOKS.COM

This is a work of fiction. Names, characters, places, and incidents either are the product of the author's imagination or are used fictitiously. Any resemblance to actual persons, living or dead, is coincidental.

Edited by David Carpenter.

Cover photo, FPG International.
Cover and Book Design by Duncan Campbell.

Printed and bound in Canada at Houghton Boston, Saskatoon.

National Library of Canada Cataloguing in Publication Data

Helgason, Gail, date-
Swimming into darkness

ISBN 1-55050-186-0

1. Title.
PS8565.E4534S94 2001   C813'.54   C2001-911220-3
PR9199.3.H4447S94 2001

1   2   3   4   5   6   7   8   9   10

COTEAU BOOKS
401-2206 Dewdney Ave.
Regina, Saskatchewan
Canada   S4R 1H3

AVAILABLE IN THE U.S. FROM
General Distribution Services
4500 Witmer Industrial Estates
Niagara Falls, NY 14305-1386

The publisher gratefully acknowledges the financial assistance of the Saskatchewan Arts Board, the Canada Council for the Arts, the Government of Canada through the Book Publishing Industry Development Program (BPIDP), and the City of Regina Arts Commission, for its publishing program.

Dedicated to my Icelandic-Canadian forebears,
pioneers in Ontario, Manitoba, and Saskatchewan:
Helgi Sigurdsson and Gudbjorg Sveinsdottir; Kristjan Johann
Helgason and Halldora Johannesdottir; Hinrik Gislason
and Jorunn Magnusdottir; Stephan Olafson and
Gudrun Hinnriksdottir; Ingunn (Inga) Larson; and
Abraham Larson of Stavanger

And in honour of my parents, who took me early to the water's edge;
Stefania Gudrun (Runa) Helgason
and the late Christian Norman Helgason

This much I've learned. Nobody travels alone. These lives we lead are not our own carefully deliberate journeys, but the sum of all the paths travelled by those who were here before us, one upon the other, step by step, layer upon layer. Life upon life.

— Judy Schultz, *Mamie's Children*

Friday Morning,
JUNE 19, 1998

We are here because of the lake, my father used to say. But where I live now is nowhere near the lake my father loved. Like Markus Olafsson, I'm drawn to this river, with its water chilled by glaciers on the Continental Divide, water that slices deep clefts into the soft clay banks, so that those who build houses beside it, as Markus did, never really know, season in, season out, whether this will be the year they will be defeated by the blasting forces of wind and rain and water and snow. I prefer this river because it is always in motion, always hurrying, no matter how calm the surface appears. In winter, under thick ice, gravity pushes the current onward. In summer, even the shallows are tentative, never quite at rest.

Unlike that prairie lake of my childhood, fed by deep and hidden springs, the source of the North Saskatchewan is easily traced to the glaciers and mountain valleys Markus immortalized. Its beginnings hold no mystery. I find this calming.

What I like best about the river, though, are its twists and curves and oxbows, so you are never certain what is ahead. The need for watchfulness can never be forgotten.

A prairie lake can be too translucent, too full of the sky, too dreamy, too much like a mirror. It can pretend to tell you everything and tell you nothing. It can lull you to sleep when you most need to be alert. A river like this one, heavy, silt-ridden, intricately braided with unseen currents, makes no such false promises.

Less than two weeks from now, visitors to Olafsson House will gaze at the river, tour the homestead, and learn about the miraculous life of the humble Alberta farmer who lived here. For it was nothing less than miraculous, surely, for a man, living in such conditions, working twelve hours a day in the fields, to have retired to his study in the evenings and produced the finest poetry written in the Icelandic language since the thirteenth century.

The thought of the invitations on my desk at the museum gives me a rush of pleasure. They are rather clever, really, especially considering that our communications budget isn't what it once was: cream stock, serif typeface, shaped to form the silhouette of a spinning wheel:

You are invited to attend the opening of Alberta Culture's newest historic site, the Markus Olafsson House, on Wednesday, July 1, at 2 p.m. at Edmonton's Terwillegar Park.

Direct and to the point, doubtless like Markus himself. I'll have them posted when I get back.

But first I want to have a look myself at that minor leakage Kramer mentioned in his maintenance report this morning. "Might not be too much, Thora," he'd said. "But I thought you should know."

I leave the Volvo in front of the farmstead and approach Olafsson House. The wind blows hard, picking up bits of grit from the newly planted lawn. Tiny blades of grass shine brightly after last night's rain. My staff went to some trouble to obtain that grass seed, a hybrid variety mixed with some prairie weeds and even dandelions. We've been assured the result will not appear too homogeneous or tended.

Inside, I can't help but take a moment to look approvingly at the living room, everything in place: even the piano and gramophone. I don't open the door to the study, my favourite room and certainly Markus's. But I can't resist running my hand lightly along the dark polished door. This was part of his literary tool kit, I think, as much so as his ploughs and harvester and the electric knitting machine he purchased for his wife and daughters. The door shut him in and his family out, enabling him to produce the poetry that once ranked him with Emerson and Whitman and perhaps still would, were it not for the daunting difficulties posed by English translation. They revere him still, on that little volcanic island near the Arctic Circle, although after 1874 Markus thought of himself as an Icelandic-Canadian. A "West Icelander."

It took us three years to track down his writing desk, but that was the least of our work.

And now the site is almost ready.

I pull a pencil flashlight out of my purse and open the door to the cellar, which leads off the kitchen. There's a musty smell, but not as bad as it was when we started the restoration. Discarded bags of cement and Fiberfil batt are strewn on the earthen floor. A prickle of annoyance rises in my chest. Another thing to do before July 1.

At first glance, the foundation walls appear to be doing their job. We had a sump pump installed, with a discharge pipe running out of the basement and away from the foundation. A simple system, to be sure, but certainly the most economical one.

The light traces a yellow beam along the west corner. There it is. A patch of dampness spreading like a fungus. I place my hands against the rough surface. No question. It's weeping. Christ.

Kramer's report is stuffed into the pocket of my denim skirt. He examined it two days ago. Then the damp area covered no more than a few inches. Now it's spread to more than a foot.

I try to call Kramer on my cellphone to talk about the leakage, but there is no answer. Then I permit myself a few more minutes by the river. The brown water is full of twigs, branches, and the occasional uprooted tree. Poplar fluff floats against a white glaring sky. Another warm day ahead, Environment Canada predicts. The snowpack up in the Rockies will melt like mad today.

When my father said, "We are here because of the lake," he meant because of the whitefish and the pike and the hay meadows that glistened at the edge of the marshes of that Saskatchewan lake. But I think he meant something else as well, something that must have remained hidden from him all his life. Some genetic memory of spewing ash, perhaps, igniting deep within a neural pathway?

Here, in this new land, no lava streams dammed up the lakes; no volcanoes erupted to turn day into night. Imagine Mount Robson, pulverized, and you can begin to know what it must have been like: the tiny particles turning air into stone, blocking the sun, layering the rooftops of the wooden houses and the sheds, stinging the eyes, congesting the mucous membranes. The women in Iceland clutched linen handkerchiefs in front of their nostrils to filter the clogged air; within an hour the cloth turned dark as storm clouds.

They called the last winter on that northern island the blood-winter, *blooverturinn.* Under that mountain of ash, the cold became so severe that sheep and cattle lay dying; the owners could not bear to hear their cries and bled them to death to release them from their pain.

And so my Icelandic ancestors came to this land, the precise opposite of an island. Not all ventured here, of course. Some journeyed to yet another wind-driven, barren island off Nova Scotia, some to Brazil. Many stopped briefly in Kinmount, Ontario, where the size of the timber appalled and defeated them, accustomed as they were only to the small trees and shrubs that managed to gain a toehold in the island's light and porous soil. They moved onward. The majority stopped along the shores of Lake Winnipeg, but a few ventured three hundred miles further west, taking care to avoid the treeless plains to the south. Instead they chose the aspen parkland, that narrow, rich ribbon of fertile land, mixed forest, open grassland, and rolling hills extending from southern Manitoba through central Saskatchewan to the eastern foothills of the Rockies.

Some, like Markus Olafsson, went as far west as the rich parkland on the edge of boreal forest, in the territory that became the province of Alberta. Eventually the new land swallowed him up. After all these years, his death remains as puzzling as his life.

More than a hundred years later, I followed Markus to this restless, churning water. Some would say my being here is hardly surprising. In our own ways, we both chose exile.

Saturday,
JUNE 30, 1962

Until that night, when the trouble started, I never dove deep. I preferred the shallows that stretched beyond the dock in front of my parents' cabin. Under water, as I glided along the bottom of the lake, maskless, eyes open, tunnelling through an opaque greenish brown world, my shrunken field of vision took in only what was directly ahead of and beneath me.

The slightest variation thrilled me. Tiny wave patterns sculpted the sand. Here and there in the murky water, I'd discover opalescent snail shells, worn bits of amber glass, faded beer bottle caps, a bobby pin, a rusted red-and-white spoon from some long-forgotten fishing expedition. I would clutch these objects in my fist and bob to the surface, and although I never found treasure, I swam always with its possibility.

For Gretchen McConnell, my best friend the summer I was thirteen, swimming underwater held no interest. "Everything's blurry under there," she'd say, in a matter-of-fact way. "You go in. I'll watch."

She'd wait for me on the beach, her insect morphology and botany books propped up against a sloping pile of sand she'd fashioned for her comfort with quick, abrupt movements. She admired the hard, incontestable look of chemical equations on a page, and the schematic diagrams of native prairie perennials with their hollow round stems and spikelets and blades. Even more, she loved the spanking clear line the surface of the lake made against the far shoreline on bright Saskatchewan days. She said this country was full of such sharp planes of light that she sometimes felt she'd never known what sunshine and space were until she'd moved here.

Gretchen's chemical equations meant nothing more to me than ink on a page, and most of the time when I stared across the lake and tried to see the same line as she did along the horizon, it would blend into the greenery, soft and woolly, and make my eyes hurt. Gretchen insisted the line was there, plain as anything, if I knew how to look.

Which of us had the idea for the cupcake candles? I thought it was mine – a summer diversion learned from my mother – until Gretchen claimed it as her own, saying that almost all Scottish children who lived near the sea fashioned such candles. I have since asked others from her country if they have heard of such an activity. They always say no. But at the start of that summer my doubts about Gretchen had not yet begun.

"Dip them quickly, Thora," she directed earlier that Saturday. Even then I was good at fixing dates and times, if not numbers, in my head. We hauled an old table from

Gretchen's porch out onto the beach, along with a dozen slabs of paraffin wax from my mother's canning supplies, several cartons of large Reynolds paper baking cups in rainbow colours, and a pot for melting the wax over a driftwood fire. My job was to position the baking cups on the table with tongs as Gretchen poured in the melted wax, then quickly add the wick before the wax hardened. The task was more difficult than it sounded, because the wax didn't melt evenly and tended to form messy gobs.

"More quickly," Gretchen kept saying. She tossed her pale copper hair in the breeze and with an elastic band fastened it into a ponytail before she examined my handiwork.

When we finished, she counted the candles. More than two dozen.

"It'll be beautiful," she said. "You wait. It'll be the most beautiful Dominion Day swim ever."

At the prairie lake where I spent that summer and all the summers of my youth, a midnight swim on Dominion Day had become a tradition between myself, Gretchen, and her father, whose name was Robert but who we all called Mac. He was the only doctor in the nearby town of Gilead.

Usually we did not swim late at night, which made Dominion Day special. Gretchen, in fact, claimed that swimming inland bored her. She'd proclaim that Whitefish Lake was not big enough for her, not cold enough, not *dramatic* enough. And then she'd tell me about the North Sea, how the water always looked grey as old mutton in the drizzle. Before the McConnells emigrated to Canada, she and her father insisted on celebrating birthdays by swimming in the sea, no matter what the weather. That was when they lived in Edinburgh, before Dr. McConnell had been lured to our town with its better pay and shiny new hospital and no National Health.

In Gilead, which was twelve miles south of Whitefish Lake in east-central Saskatchewan, the British doctors usually stayed a year or two, three at the most. Then they'd be off to the cities. Dr. McConnell was the exception. He'd practised in Gilead for four years by the time the difficulties began, and my parents and their friends were beginning to think that this time they'd found a doctor who would stay. None of us would have predicted that we were about to enjoy our last Dominion Day swim together.

That Saturday night Gretchen and I made a fire on the beach while we waited for Mac to return from Gilead Union Hospital. He'd said he would try to be back by midnight. But both Gretchen and I knew that this was no ordinary night, and that he'd have many patients to release and extra duties to perform.

"A strike like this has never happened before in North America," Gretchen said. "Of course it'd be nothing new in Europe."

As usual, I accepted Gretchen's pronouncements on world

events. Her comments even made me grateful; they always seemed to hold a kernel of knowledge and yet they were nothing like our Social Studies texts in school, with their family trees of the English royal family and tedious maps showing the chief sources of tin and bauxite and nickel in Canada.

"Curses," Gretchen said. She'd been trying to straighten the wick on one candle and instead broke it off.

"You weren't looking," I said. I'd seen her eyes wander up the driveway, watching for Mac.

"Yes, I was," she said, lightly. "The string must have been weak in the first place."

"I suppose."

I rocked on the sand with my knees against my chin. I thought how my words must sound to Gretchen, how hesitant and meek. My awkwardness before her never made me feel bad, because I learned things from Gretchen that I wouldn't have learned from other girls, whimsical, beautiful things, things you could turn and tip over and over in your mind and still find something new. Gretchen knew all the constellations of the northern sky and the speed at which giraffes gallop; when she talked about such things her voice became rapturous, the way other girls did when the new Eaton's winter catalogue arrived in the mail.

It was twenty to one in the morning when the Buick pulled up on the McConnells' driveway. I remember because I looked at the waterproof watch my parents had bought for my birthday the month before. It was a Timex with a Mickey Mouse face that rather embarrassed me. I'd asked for it for my twelfth birthday and received it on my thirteenth. Secretly I hoped that if I wore the watch underwater long enough, some trickles of moisture would seep into a crack and dissolve the mouse's face. I bore Mickey no grudge; part of me simply acknowledged that the difference between twelve and thirteen was greater than he could span.

I would not have dreamed of damaging the watch myself. I still subscribed to the soothing belief that merely hoping for something to happen frequently caused it to happen, without undue effort on my part. My parents called this praying. I thought of it as magic.

Certainly only magic could have brought Gretchen to Gilead. Even now, I find it difficult to say what she meant to me. Without her, I would surely have been as solitary as the tree-perching sandpiper that roosted in the woods behind my parents' summer cabin, always staying off by itself, unlike the plovers and other sandpipers that flocked to the shore each spring and fall.

Both she and I were the same age that summer, about to enter Grade Nine in the fall, still growing into our skins. We were a year younger than others in our grade: Gretchen pushed ahead by the excellence of the Scottish school system, myself by the results of scholastic aptitude tests. These results had prompted my Grade Seven teacher to petition my parents and the school superintendent to allow me to skip ahead a year. The schoolwork in the advanced grade seemed as easy to me as it had before, except for the math and science. But I was aware of other difficulties. I was too young to wear lipstick as many of the other girls in Grade Eight did, and unlike them, I had no need to wear a bra.

I f it was true that Gretchen and I didn't have many other friends, we barely noticed at the time.

We must have made an unusual pair. Me, Thora Sigurdson, thin-boned, lanky, hair the colour of straw, shorn in a choppy pixie cut, and my perpetual peeling sunburns, my whiteheads, my bare feet, my ragtag way of doing things that always seemed to work out, mostly, I suspected, because I took care not to attempt tasks at which I might fail. And Gretchen, chunky-shouldered, thick-waisted, and fussy, with her letter-perfect notebooks, oxford shoes polished nightly, a sharpened pencil above one ear to keep track of what she called her "observations," which that summer centred on the clear-winged grasshopper. She had fine-grained skin, white as rice from nine years in Scotland, dull copper hair, rather imperti-nent brown eyes, luminous and unsettling, a strong promi-nent jaw, and a firmness of view combined with an odd reserve that, I later discovered, is not uncommon in well-behaved, exceptionally intelligent females. Everything about her seemed commanding and composed.

Gretchen never boasted of her accomplishments. She didn't have to. I was the one who did that.

"Did you know," I might say in passing to someone like Rosemary Krywulak, who lived next door to me at the lake, sixteen and her nose stuck in *Seventeen* magazines and books like *Forever Amber,* "Gretchen's out in Vancouver now, for the National Youth Science Fair?" Or "Gretchen learned to read when she was four. Her father taught her."

Saying such words made me proud, as if some of the glory could bounce back. Not for me the detailed log work that kept Gretchen up at night, counting fruit fly pupae and examining the social behavior of aphids and ants. I was too lazy to try to win scholarships myself, and I'd already realized I could get Bs and a smattering of As without often bringing school books home.

What I see now is that I could absorb Gretchen's energy, but I couldn't deflect it. We needed each other, because in the heat of adolescence there are kinds of energy that are good for you and other kinds that can burn you up, and until that summer we fuelled the first kind in each other.

"Sorry I'm late, lassies," Mac said. His feet made pleasant sifting sounds against the sand. He'd already changed into swim trunks and wore nothing else although the night was cool.

Only a few stubborn coals still glowed from the fire. He reached down for a twig, snap-snap-snapped it into small sections and placed them over the coals. They burst into spitting flames.

"What's this, then?" He picked at the remains of the damaged candle that Gretchen had thrown back into the fire.

She looked at me.

"Nothing," she said.

Mac was a tall, well-built man in his late thirties, springy as coiled brass. He reminded me of a movie hero of mine at the time, Dirk Bogarde, with his jet-black hair and knowing expression. His hair was luxuriant, pushed back straight from his forehead, and his movements always seemed controlled, as if he were struggling to contain the kinetic energy under his skin. He had a way of tossing his head back that some took to be arrogance, but which I think was confidence. He'd had acne in his youth, so his complexion still held a trace of scarring, and his dark brown eyes always seemed alert like those of the rich American goose hunters who swarmed to the marshlands along the lake each fall. Yet he also possessed a curiously distracted air where certain practical matters were concerned. He never seemed to notice, for example, the lengthening column of ash on the end of his cigarettes, and he was forever scattering ash over the floors and dining room tables of Gilead.

Mac spoke in an even tone and had, by my mother's high standards, the most gracious manners of anyone she had ever met. He made it his practice to swim across the lake one day each summer, a distance of some nine miles, a feat that no one else in the entire area had ever attempted.

"Are you actually on strike now?" Gretchen asked. It was the same tone she might have used to inquire if a patient she'd recently seen alive had really died.

"That's what they tell me," Mac said. He was not an especially talkative man. He pushed sand onto the fire in slow, careful motions, as if burying our words. "Shall we proceed then, ladies? Give Canada our special Happy Birthday greeting?"

"We're ready," said Gretchen. "We've got our bathing suits on underneath."

We couldn't see much of the lake, but we could hear the soft lap of waves on the beach. The water pulled me like a black liquid magnet. There were plenty of lakes in this part of the province, but none were as large as Whitefish, or favoured with as many fine beaches.

Distant lights of cabins flickered from Walema Beach on the other side of the lake. Stars shivered against the deep black prairie sky. Saskatoon, the closest city, was one hundred and fifty miles west.

Our beach, West Beach, formed part of a wide bay that swung out to the Gilead Co-operative Public Beach on one side and a shrubby rock-strewn point, Peter's Point, on the other. The cabins stretched on either side of us. Most had been hauled there or built on the ridge overlooking the beach in the last two or three years. They seemed to sit uneasily, as if stealing time from the never-ending cycle of tasks that occupied their owners, large-scale wheat farmers from around Gilead mostly, or people who made their living indirectly from agriculture in those days of the massive Russian grain sales: the Royal Bank manager, the Credit Union manager, the owners of the Red & White, the dry goods store, the dry cleaning plant.

Each of the cabins stood just at the point where the firm

subsoil gave way to one of the longest, sandiest beaches in Saskatchewan. "And this is a province large enough to swallow all of Britain, including Scotland," I liked to remind Gretchen. "You really should see Loch Ness," she'd say. "It's a different kind of beauty, entirely. Wild, but in a somewhat more manageable sense."

My father, Bjorn Sigurdson, and Mac had purchased the leases for West Beach three springs previously from a local farmer who had used the land to pasture cattle. They hired a man to bulldoze the scrub grass and dwarf poplar and Russian sow thistle along the shore between Peter's Point and the public beach. After we burned the brush in a big bonfire, the beach had been raked and harrowed. When people in Gilead saw how fine the sand was under all those weeds and brush, they bought up the rest of the lots in one summer. My father and Mac kept the prices reasonable; Mac said the main thing was to get people out to enjoy the lake.

Darkness sealed the cabin next door, which belonged to my parents. I could well imagine my mother, whose name was Jonina, and my father wrapped up tight for the night under their tattered horsehide. Most of the cabins were unoccupied. Some still had their windows boarded up. School had only been out for a few days; CBC Radio 540 in Regina said most people were staying as close to home as they could this Dominion Day weekend because of the impending medical crisis.

No fireworks had been set off by the lake that night to mark the beginning of the holiday. In our province, individuals were not permitted to purchase fireworks and no organizations had bothered. The only illumination shone from the yardlight at the end of the McConnells' driveway. Gretchen's mother, Alexia, had gone to bed hours before. She was an artist and liked to rise early to paint in the morning light.

The cool glare imprinted the shadow of the flagpole on the foot-trodden sand.

"Just a minute," Mac said.

He walked back to the flagpole, unwrapped the flag and hoisted it halfway up. His amiable face shone under the electric light, as if illuminated from within. I couldn't stop watching him. His eyes followed the progress of the flag up the pole with such concentration that he seemed to be willing it to rise.

"Do you need to do that now?" Gretchen called.

"Yes," he said, in a cheerful tone. "As a matter of fact, I do."

When Mac relaxed at the lake, which was as often as he could in summer, he always watched for the flag. If he was out swimming, or fishing, and the hospital called or a patient needed him, up went the flag and before long he would come. When the flag was at half-mast, we all knew he was either at the cabin or on the beach, but not on the water. If it was down, it meant he was at the hospital or his house in Gilead.

"I thought you were off duty for a while," Gretchen said. Her voice skidded in a way I hadn't heard before.

Together we walked down to the water. The sand was icy on my bare feet. I wrapped a towel around me and

stopped at the edge. Mac was not usually one to hesitate. "A
man who can't sit still," my father said of him. "A real jumping
bean." That night Mac began to kick a channel in the sand, as
a child might.

Gretchen shivered beside me. She didn't really like swimming; she liked what she called historic occasions.

"That's really the problem with Canada, I think," she said
once. "There isn't enough history. It's like a baby in diapers as
far as countries go. So you have to invent your own traditions."

I seemed to be the only one aching to be in the water.

"Let's get in," I said, and started to push the wooden rowboat down to the lake. The small, wide-bottomed craft,
painted hunter green, had been bought second-hand for
Gretchen, mostly to save wear and tear on the speedboat lov-
ingly housed in the boat shed.

The boat's bottom scraped against the sand. Together we
manoeuvred it into the water, which felt warmer than the
night air. The shallows stretched so far that you had to be
careful not to run aground before you started. That was why
so many cabin owners had built long docks that protruded
like huge wooden teeth into the bay.

When the water reached our knees, we each slipped into
the boat. I got in first and Gretchen carefully handed me the
cookie sheet with the cupcake candles. Mac rowed with firm,
jolting strokes. The glide of the boat, the creak of the oars,
and the splash of water were the only sounds on the lake.

In a few minutes we reached the diving platform. Mac had

built it two years before, so the kids on West Beach could have a deep, safe place to dive and jump. We all called it "the raft," because that was what it most resembled, a large planked raft, with a low diving board on one end and a high tower board on the other. The year before it was built, a young boy from town had been seriously injured when he dove off the end of a dock into the shallows.

Mac brought the boat parallel to the raft and Gretchen and I got off. The platform leaned slightly with our weight. Gretchen held the side of the boat while her father alighted and secured the painter.

Usually on Dominion Day we dove off the raft simultaneously, then quickly got back in the boat and paddled back to shore, bones tingling. But that night Gretchen set the cookie sheet out on the raft and lit each candle. The tiny flames glowed in the calm air.

I had thought that the three of us would divide the candles evenly, each setting our portion afloat. But Gretchen's hands flew in her efficient way, so that before I realized what she had done, all the candles danced in the water in a yellow and orange blaze. She must have been so intent on what she was doing that she'd forgotten Mac and I might also enjoy setting some adrift. A couple of the candles had already gone out, I noticed with satisfaction.

"There," Gretchen said. "Isn't that super?"

The lights bobbed on the black silk water, and as they moved farther away from the raft, the flames seemed to burn brighter, some clustering into large glowing bulbs and others dispersing from the rest into liquid blackness.

"Happy Birthday, Canada," Gretchen said.

"Let's get in for our swim," I said. The blood pulsed at my wrist. The lights from the candles were pretty, but they had everything to do with Gretchen and nothing to do with me. Mac stood at the edge of the raft, motionless. Gretchen turned reluctantly away from the sight of the candles. She rubbed her shoulders and shivered. That's the way I remember things, anyway.

I waited for someone else to make the first move. I was accustomed to doing what I was told, partly because I was too indolent to make my own decisions. Being around Gretchen made things easy for me, because with the exception of her science experiments and my fondness for swimming underwater, we usually wanted to do the same things.

I think too that I still held in my memory the expression on Mac's face when he had hoisted the flag. There'd been a jubilance in his eyes, combined with a defiance, and it was as though the airwaves of that dark night had transmitted some of his defiance through my sluggish skin, and I knew then that he would have understood about the Mickey Mouse watch if I had told him, although my parents certainly wouldn't have. I didn't know until then that responsible adults could break rules, with relish, and I recognized that the relish in Mac's face could become our secret.

It also came to me, although I could not have said how, that Mac was waiting for some act that would separate this night from others like it, and that Gretchen's way, imaginative and lovely as it had been, had not been enough.

"Let's race," I said. A picture like nothing else I'd seen came into my mind: myself, sliding with ease through the beamless depths, effortlessly parting slithery curtains of weeds. Beating both of them to shore.

"Come on," I said. "Let's all swim back underwater. We can tie up the boat and swim out for it tomorrow."

Even as my mouth formed the words, my chest constricted. Gretchen hated swimming underwater.

"Good idea," Mac said. "Okay, Gretch?"

"It's different from what we've done other years," she said. "But okay."

"We'll swim side by side," Mac said. "I'll come back for the boat."

My toes curled over the edge of the raft. Mac was in the middle.

"You have to just plunge in," Gretchen said. "It's the only way."

"One, two, three, go," Mac cried.

We dove in. The water pressed around my skin like a warm bath. It wasn't greenish, only black. I couldn't see Mac or Gretchen, and I didn't care. I was in a tunnel, and for once I knew exactly where I had come from and exactly where I was going. For so long I'd been afraid of this tunnel, this world of deep water, and now that I was immersed, it seemed to hold me in a tepid, friendly clasp. Gretchen could take the candles away from me, but she'd never be able to take away this sensation.

My chest started to burn, but I kept on swimming, a

breaststroke, long and smooth and even. Masses of slithery vegetation pulled at the edges of my skin. I couldn't touch the bottom, but I knew I was close to it, and that by the time I surfaced my lungs would burn so badly I'd be afraid my chest would tear open.

Mac and Gretchen would be proud of me. They knew my fear of the depths.

The vegetation thinned. The water turned lighter brown. The surface seemed to draw me up. I reached the ridge of the shallows, left the weeds behind, and stood up on firm, clean sand.

Mac and Gretchen were about ten feet behind me, each doing an easy crawl. A hollow feeling came into my throat when I realized that they hadn't swum underwater at all. They'd let me go ahead and then they'd cheated.

I could see Mac holding himself back, but I sensed something else too. A hesitation in the way Gretchen moved through the water, as if she was trying not to touch it and to move through it at the same time.

As they approached, I waited to hear the silvery sounds of their congratulations. Mac stood up first, then Gretchen. She shook her head vigorously, lightly splashing my skin. The drops felt like sun-heated pebbles. I shivered.

"That was well done, lass," Mac said. For a moment I thought he was speaking to me. But when I turned around, he was looking at Gretchen. At least, that's the way I remember it.

"Look," she said.

The candles were tiny pinpoints of light now, beaming

through the darkness. They grew smaller as we watched. Looking at the candles intensified the feeling of disorientation I'd experienced since I surfaced. I stepped up to the yardlight to finish towelling myself off. There was no use waiting for Gretchen to congratulate me. A bitter taste came into my mouth, as if I'd swallowed sand.

Tuesday,
JULY 3, 1962

My daydreams always seemed to be disordered then; they split apart from me like firewood on the beach when I tried to carry too large a load for a campfire. They tumbled and clattered around me and sometimes they sent slivers into my flesh, as if trying to fool me into thinking they were real.

I was daydreaming at the end of my father's dock when Rosemary, one of the Krywulak twins, approached. Dominion Day had been cool and rainy and I'd gone back with my parents to our house in Gilead where we lived most of the year. I hadn't seen Gretchen since the night swim. The morning after, I'd woken with the persistent feeling that a fine chain had been wrapped around me in my sleep, a chain that twisted around my throat and my chest and my hips and knees and ankles, and would take all my strength and cunning to break. Such a silly daydream. It meant nothing at all.

"We need a third," Rosemary said. "I suddenly realized you're probably old enough. My sister doesn't think you are, but I do."

Rosemary had one of those voices, deep and modulated, that encircled you wherever you were. She was short and thin, with fine, medium-length hair fair as the foxtail that grew in profusion along the lake's marshy bays. Hers were the kind of looks that fashion magazines such as *Ingenue* called pert. One of her front teeth was slightly crooked, which gave her a perpetually playful look. What I remember best is her habit of standing with her legs planted slightly apart, like stubborn poles, and at the same time the impression she conveyed of endless springiness and bounce. Rosemary had won the gymnastics medal at the district meet the spring before. She could do the splits.

I didn't answer right away. I pretended to peer through binoculars at the fishing boats strung out along Peter's Point like snap-together plastic beads. I wasn't accomplishing anything, and I liked that. I wanted to catch the fading shimmer of another daydream before Rosemary's voice grounded me. I managed to retain only the glimpse of a palazzo dance floor and a tulle net gown and a slim white-gold watch. Curlicues of imitation roses adorned either side of the diamond-shaped face, where thin black lines, delicate as a cat's whiskers, substituted for numbers.

The air seemed too fresh for July, and the sky glowed with an eerie brightness that hurt my eyes, as if trying to make up for the fact that it wasn't blue. Somewhere out on the lake, my parents competed in the annual Whitefish Lake Derby. The public beach was almost deserted, although my Mickey Mouse watch told me it was almost noon.

Rosemary looked surprised when I didn't jump right away at the chance to ski. She'd pegged me as a follower, I realized, and this time the thought rankled. Once the previous spring she had picked me as her jiving partner. This was in the school basement where older girls danced during recess to scratched singles like "Honeycomb" and "Wake Up Little Susie." Gretchen and I had gone down to "observe," as she put it. And then Rosemary had grabbed my hand and twirled me around until I was light-headed. When she danced, she radiated energy; she moved so fast, all the charms on her cheap gold bracelet blurred into one.

"You've got rhythm," she'd laughed. She'd given me a little curtsy, like a princess, and propelled me back to the wall where Gretchen stood watching.

"I'm still dizzy," I'd said, as Gretchen and I climbed up the back stairs to class. My steps were light with the pleasure of having been singled out.

"Poor you," Gretchen said. "Did you know your crinoline's showing?"

A whining noise split the air.

I looked back at the cabins.

Trust Vivienne Krywulak. She was trying to start a gas lawn mower. No one else at the lake even bothered trying to tend a lawn out here; that was town work that they came out to their cabins to avoid.

But Vivienne seemed to have brought the town with her, in a way. She often wore high-heeled shoes when she walked

down to the beach, her hair in a tight home perm, and sometimes, late at night, I could hear music from her hi-fi coming
through the open windows. Usually the music she played was
sugary and sweet, and slightly behind times. Patti Page most
likely.

That summer, Vivienne and her twin daughters, Rosemary
and Arlene, had rented the cabin on the other side of the one
owned by my parents. I didn't really know them well; the
twins were sixteen and would be starting Grade Eleven that
year, two grades ahead of Gretchen and me. They'd moved to
our town two years before from a village between Yorkton and
Gilead, a village so small the girls had to take the school bus
to Gilead Composite High School, a round trip of one and a
half hours each way.

Where their father was no one seemed to know. Vivienne
had found a job as a receptionist for Mac, but that hadn't
lasted long. Now she worked in the poultry eviscerating plant
at the edge of town and was said to spend time with Jerry
Embury, one of the school bus drivers who used to work for
my Uncle Gisli. The plant was Gilead's only industry.
Vivienne did some heavy cleaning for my mother once in a
while, scrubbing kitchen walls or shampooing the rugs.
Sometimes after she'd been at our house, I thought I could
still smell her presence, a mixture of white lilac toilet water
and baby oil and chicken shit and grease and feathers. I did
not find this smell unpleasant. There was a forcefulness to it
that I liked, a lack of apology.

"So, cutie-pie," Rosemary called again. "Are you coming?"

A horsefly landed on her leg. She snapped at it ferociously with her beach towel, but she must have only stunned it, because the horsefly continued to buzz around her in jerky circles.

"What for?" I asked. It was true that I liked to follow, but I also liked to have reasons.

"It should be good," Rosemary said. "Almost everyone's at the fishing derby. We should have the whole bay to ourselves. Maybe we could even get Clement to let us do a braid."

"Okay, okay," I said to Rosemary. "I'm coming."

"Good."

Before that moment, I hadn't thought of myself as the kind of person who would ever have the nerve to do a braid.

I stood up and gripped my plastic thongs hard with my toes.

"Yeah," I said to Rosemary. "Maybe we can."

Usually I skied alone. I invented my own way to do tricks, like skiing backwards or slipping the handle of the tow rope between my thighs, then flapping my arms and shouting, "No hands," as if anyone could hear me. I performed these tricks at a fairly slow speed behind my father's boat or Mac's. Almost anyone could have done them at such speeds. But from the beach, viewers lost perspective on speed. I'd been told that I appeared confident, even daring, skiing on that lake. It was the only place I did, although since Dominion Day I'd begun to think that could change.

We walked north toward Clement's, Rosemary beside me, Arlene slightly behind. In a way I thought of Arlene as a hangnail, colourless, not really alive, but clinging and irritating. As usual, she had her head down. She didn't talk or laugh as much as Rosemary, and when she did, she usually only addressed her sister.

Away from Rosemary, Arlene wouldn't have been noticed in a crowd. She was darker and heavier, with hair the colour of weak tea and a penchant for loose-fitting shifts, and if it hadn't been for her quick, intelligent eyes and strong, muscled arms and legs, she might have been thought of as lumpish. Once in a while I saw her in the Gilead Public Library, always in the history and politics section where I never ventured. Even though she took out thick books, her schoolmates said she rarely spoke out in class, and then only in Social Studies. She reminded me of the sundogs that glowed on either side of the sun on cold days in winter, pale and vapourish, holding no possibility of warmth. My mother said the sundogs meant that colder weather was on its way. Yet the sundogs could be impish and beautiful. Sometimes they'd fade in front of your eyes and you'd wonder if you'd seen anything at all. When I'd been younger, I'd thought of them as Jack Frost's ghosts. I didn't think of Arlene as either impish or beautiful, but I recognized in her the same cool ability to transform herself, and that recognition made me uneasy.

Gretchen and I weren't like Rosemary and Arlene, and until that summer I never dreamed I'd ever want to be. Twice that week the twins had sat on our dock energetically scrubbing their feet and smoothing out the hard ridges under their big toes with pumice stones. They painted their toenails coral and white pearl, and sunned while the paint dried, wads of cotton batten stuck between each toe. A few hardened drops speckled the dock.

The McConnells' Buick swung up to their driveway. Figures clambered out. Of course. Tuesday was the morning Gretchen monitored grasshoppers in a nearby hay meadow. She'd undertaken a study of the clear-winged grasshopper, comparing growth patterns in dry and wet conditions. We'd had mostly hot, dry weather, and the grasshopper menace in Saskatchewan was said to be the worst since the thirties, a condition that was the cause for some glee on Gretchen's part.

Gretchen had asked if I could help her on Tuesday mornings with her hopper monitoring. But that morning I forgot. At least I think I forgot. My mind had started being fuzzy about such things those first days in July, and as time went on, I sometimes suspected that there were things I was remembering to forget, maybe even things I still haven't remembered.

"You girls my only takers?" Clement Hummel shouted over the noise of the Merc 85-horse outboard. "Can't you find one more? It's perfect out there for a foursome."

He smiled out of the side of his mouth. Clement was about forty, a man who made a small living repairing motors and welding farm equipment. But most of the summer he was out on the water. He didn't fish, didn't swim, didn't sun. What he did was pull water-skiers: all ages, all abilities, always for free and always obligingly. Whitefish Lake was Clement's stage and he the choreographer.

"Our own aquatic version of Celia Franca," Mac had called him.

I think now that the doctor was onto something; surely it was only on the water that someone like Clement Hummel could ever be at the centre of action on the beach. That was what the lake did for a lot of us. It evened things out. You could be nothing on terra firma and competent and graceful and brave out on the water. Or you could be adroit and brave on terra firma, and a complete dolt on the water. And it wasn't a matter of skill, exactly, or luck, or having the money to buy a little boat or a big boat. It had more to do with the kind of thoughts you took with you, as if all that expanse of water could erase your land thoughts. I think, for example, that the way Clement thought on the water, gunning his big boat and calling the shots, was nothing like the way he thought on shore, where he seemed grateful to do the most menial task, like digging out long stubborn roots of black poplar on the beach for my father and Mac.

And the way Gretchen thought when she swam in Whitefish Lake must have been nothing like the way she thought when she was immersed in the biting cold of the North Sea. She made the mistake of thinking the lake wasn't formidable enough for her, like an equestrian who underestimates a small but sprightly horse.

"So whaddya think?" Clement asked again.

"We can only get three today, Clement," Rosemary said. She strapped on a lifebelt from the pile on the dock. She'd selected a flattering waist-belt style and pulled it tight, so her waist looked skinnier and her bust looked bigger. I picked out a bulky chest jacket stuffed with kapok; my parents had stressed that chest jackets were safer than the waist-belt style.

I liked skiing in foursomes, because that number encouraged the dancelike weavings and turnings that appealed to me. Sometimes skiers in foursomes could fan out so far across the water that they left a wake as foamy and frilled as a lacy fan, and for a long time after they'd finished skiing, the outlines of that fan would be visible on the surface of the lake, as subtle and light as Oriental brushwork.

My eyes wandered up to the McConnells' cabin again. The white flag was at half-mast, which meant that Mac was still there or on the beach somewhere, although I couldn't see any sign of him or Gretchen or Alexia.

"I could probably get Gretchen," I said.

Arlene had her back to me and was fumbling amidst the life jackets.

"Sure," Rosemary said. "You're best friends, right?"

I nodded. The zipper on my jacket wouldn't catch.

"It's not quite as fast skiing with four," Rosemary said. "And of course we couldn't do a braid. But if that's what you want, it's fine with me."

Clement was standing up in the boat, unravelling the tow lines that he carefully checked and coiled each day. A breeze worked itself up, blowing choppy little waves into what had been a ceramic-smooth surface a few minutes before. The ragged clouds were smoke-grey around the edges. The air carried the vaguest scent of rain.

"On the other hand," I said, "it'd be fun to do a braid."

"Suit yourself," Rosemary said.

"It's to be a braid, ladies?" Clement asked.

"Yes," I said. The zipper finally caught. "Make it a braid."

He sat down on his vinyl driver's seat and began shortening two of the three tow ropes so each would be a slightly different length.

There wasn't enough room on the dock for three persons to do a dry start, so we all pushed ourselves into the water. As usual on sunless days, the lake was warmer than the air. Rosemary and Arlene were already squeezing their feet into the gum rubber bindings.

"Don't put me in the middle, okay?" I asked. "Let me be on either the right or left side."

I had no desire to be squeezed like a sandwich between Rosemary and Arlene.

"Actually," said Arlene, in her slow, deliberate way, "don't you think you'd be better in the middle? It's the easiest position. The rope's the shortest there."

"All right."

I pushed the skis ahead and did a lazy breaststroke. The skis were varnished wood, smooth and shiny. The anticipated adventure stretched out like a blue silk carpet in my mind. I liked to water-ski; it required little thought and no direction. You simply gave yourself to the will of the driver and your own instincts. Success depended on smooth transitions and defying the usual rules of gravity. Sometimes the more you leaned, the better your chances of staying upright.

The engine roared, the tips of the skis wobbled and then steadied, and we were off. The wind rushed against my face. I raised myself from the squatting position of my water-start and glanced at Rosemary on my left and Arlene on my right, flesh-coloured streaks in my peripheral vision.

Arlene waved to signal that we should begin the braid.

A water-ski braid consisted of intertwining the ropes of three skiers in proper sequence, much as a length of hair is braided. At the end of the ski, the tradition at the lake was to measure how much of the rope any group of skiers managed to braid in one outing. The record on the beach was about eighteen inches, a feat accomplished the year before by the twins and a cousin of theirs from Saskatoon. I'd heard that some boys on the beach were betting against anyone being able to surpass that record this summer.

The wind wrapped around my body like cellophane. Exaltation filled my veins. I could do more than walk on water, I could race on water.

As Clement turned the boat, Arlene sped in front of me. She angled her skis over the wake to the right, and then she leaned hard to her left. In one lightning movement, she edged her skis behind Rosemary, who was now on the far left.

My turn. I swung as far as I could to the left. When Clement started another circle, I lifted the rope to maintain the tension and tried to cut through the wake at a right angle to the boat, so I could slip behind Arlene.

But with my rope so short, I didn't have the play I needed to make a tight turn. I was heading right into Arlene.

I retreated to the left side. I'd have to try again.

I leaned further right to make sure I could slip behind Arlene. And then I could see that she had lied to me. There was no room for latitude. The rope was too tight, too unforgiving.

The skier in the middle didn't have the easiest position in creating a braid. Not by a long shot.

I placed all my weight on my right ski and executed the sharpest turn I'd ever made. For a moment it seemed I was going to roll into the lake with the force of a giant oil drum bouncing on pavement. And then, maybe because I still hadn't learned to fight gravity, but went with it like an autumn leaf in a gale, I managed to stay upright and slipped easily into place behind Arlene.

Clement pointed his thumb up. The skier's success signal.

I permitted myself one glance at the beach. From the water, the cabins looked like drab toy blocks. I knew I'd arrived at a place I'd never been before, a place that Gretchen had never been and perhaps never would be, and the feeling in my chest reminded me of the time I had jived with Rosemary in the school basement. I was light-headed and hot and cold at the same time, and my arms ached.

Rosemary pointed her index finger. One more time, she signalled. One more time, and faster.

Clement accelerated. The water sped under my feet faster than ever; my arm muscles felt as if tacks were being driven into them.

Rosemary wove behind me. Arlene expertly sliced the water behind us both so that she was in the middle.

I leaned left and started a quick traverse across the wake behind Rosemary, and as I did, the back of my right ski smashed into the tails of both her skis.

I crashed headfirst into the water, down and down, and then popped up. I hadn't fastened the jacket tight enough, and the top of it floated around my ears.

Clement slowed the engine and Arlene, still holding onto the tow rope, gently sank into the water.

Where was Rosemary?

I turned about in all directions but saw no sign of her.

Clement picked up one ski from the water and turned towards me. I spotted another ski a few yards ahead and started swimming towards it. I was just about to grab for the ski when it moved.

"Christ!"

Rosemary's voice, sputtering. There she was, clinging to the tail of the ski, her head so low in the water I hadn't even seen her. The water had turned her blond hair muskrat brown, and there was blood on her hands.

"You okay?" I asked.

"My leg's bleeding like hell. A ski hit me when I fell. You okay, cutie-pie?"

"Yes. Sorry. I guess that was my fault."

"Don't have kittens. You ever do a braid before?"

I didn't answer.

"Didn't think so," Rosemary said. "I kind of admire that."

I sputtered at the unexpected generosity of this remark, humiliated as I was not only by my lack of waterskiing ability, but also by my inability to be honest about it. The role of the injured and the wronged, I had thought, was to lash out and rail and reprimand, if only for the purpose of education. I was well accustomed to such reprimands from Gretchen, gently couched though they usually were. It had not occurred to me before that moment that being less than forthright could ever be considered laudable. Perhaps, I realized, such action could even – from a certain angle – be interpreted as bravery.

Clement manoeuvred the boat as close as he could.

"Her leg's hurt," I called.

He hoisted Rosemary into the boat, then picked up Arlene and me. The slash on Rosemary's right leg extended almost the length of her calf. The blood appeared as bright as geranium petals against the metallic greyness of the sky and water.

"Here," Clement said. He threw her some bandages from his first aid kit and turned the boat towards shore. Arlene tore the bandages open with wet fingers and pressed them against her sister's leg. Blood continued to ooze out.

"I thought you said it would be easier in the middle," I said to Arlene.

She didn't answer.

What happened next comes into my head in different sequences, at different times, like one of those crazy daydreams I was always having. Often I think that I wasn't really on the beach at all that day, but watching from the distance, the way I spied on people through my binoculars from the enclosed safety of my parents' cabin.

But of course I was there. I wasn't at all removed from what happened. I can remember everything about that summer so clearly, although once in a while I even wonder about that. Is my memory of that time really as good as I think it is?

Rosemary stayed calm when we reached the dock. I'm sure of that. Arlene helped her out and carefully rewrapped the bandages, which were already starting to unravel and were stained with blood.

"I feel a little dizzy," Rosemary said.

"Don't worry," said Clement. "We'll take you right up to the doc's."

And then Rosemary's mother, Vivienne Krywulak, appeared on the dock. Her plastic flip-flops thudded on the wide planks. The heels were worn thin, I noticed, beaten down by her weight. And yet she was skinny, with knobby elbows and a bony hollow on her throat above her collarbone.

She must have been watching us as she mowed her pathetic little lawn.

"What goes on here?" she asked, in a flat tone, as if she'd been expecting this all along. She was about forty-five, with a deep suntan, skin glossy with baby oil, tight curls hugging her head. She always looked a bit shellacked to me, except for her surprisingly delicate mouth, and the funny way she had of seeming half-strong and half-shrinking.

Rosemary looked up.

"My leg," she said. "It really hurts. I think I need stitches."

"I told her the best thing to do is just to go up to the doc's," said Clement. "Just get it cleaned up properly."

Vivienne stared at him and then at Rosemary. "Let me see," she said, and opened the bandages gently. Rosemary didn't say anything, but the muscles around her mouth tightened.

"We'll take you out to Mary Gilbert's," Vivienne said. "She'll fix us up."

At first none of us said anything. I was aware that Clement had stopped unloading gear from the boat.

Mary Gilbert was an assistant to Dr. Heath, the veterinarian for the rural municipality of Gilead. She lived on a farm on the road between Whitefish Lake and Gilead, and made frequent calls at the eviscerating plant where she must have made Vivienne's acquaintance.

Clement stepped out of the boat and approached Vivienne. "Gilbert's a bloody horse and chicken doctor," he protested. "You could just run the girl up to Dr. McConnell's. Flag's half up."

We all knew there was no point in taking Rosemary to

Gilead Union Hospital. Since the strike had started on Dominion Day, only a handful of hospitals had remained open in Saskatchewan, and only for emergencies. Gilead Union Hospital wasn't one of them.

"Or else," Clement went on, "the Teasdale Hospital is open for emergencies."

"That's seventy-five miles," Vivienne said. "Come on, Rosemary." She bent down and started to help her daughter to her feet.

"I know for sure Dr. McConnell's home," I said. "I could get him."

"He's on strike, like the bloody lot of them," Vivienne said. "I won't give the greedy bastard the pleasure of refusing me."

I wanted to say that of course he wouldn't refuse her. I'd never known Mac to refuse anyone. But the words didn't come.

Vivienne and Arlene started to walk down the dock with Rosemary in between them.

I could run to the McConnells' that minute, I thought. I could run and tell Mac. He'd come. I knew he would come.

But my legs wouldn't move. There'd been a fierceness in Vivienne's eyes that I didn't want to defy. I could tell that she knew exactly where she wanted to go, and because I rarely did, and was only good at following, that was what I did, with my eyes. I watched as they hobbled up the beach to their cabin, and although I couldn't see Vivienne's Chevy, I heard the grind of the engine starting, and sometimes in the night I still hear that sound.

Only then did I notice that I was still wearing a soaking

wet life jacket. I took it off and stared up at Mac's flag. The picture windows of the McConnells' cabin reminded me of dead eyes. I wanted to hide and wished that my father and Mac had left more shrubbery on the beach.

Halfway back to my parents' cabin, it occurred to me that in all the excitement, no one had measured the length of the braid.

Wednesday Morning,
JULY 4, 1962

"Wait!" Alexia McConnell called out the morning after Rosemary's accident.

My parents and I waited in the boat as she ran down the beach towards us. She couldn't seem to grasp the toeholds on her Italian leather sandals properly and kept losing one and having to go back for it.

"Son of a gun," said my father. He idled the engine and swung the boat around to face the beach. I was still getting used to seeing him at leisure at this time of day. Most summers of my life his usual seat had been on a Massey-Harris tractor. He was a broad-shouldered man of sixty-four with dull grey hair, relaxed blue eyes and skin cross-hatched with wrinkles. He had small hands, for a man, hands that were graceful in their movements and smelled of Lifebuoy soap. It seemed strange and wonderful that he could be with my mother and me these summer mornings. At the same time, a threat hovered on the fringes of all our enjoyment. I simply tried not to think about my father's heart condition.

My parents and I had just been setting off from the dock. It was about ten o'clock on the fourth day of the Saskatchewan doctors' strike. My mother sat on one of the back seats with an expression of utter calm on her face. She'd wrapped a white gauze scarf around her head and knotted it under her chin, in the brisk, neat manner of Queen Elizabeth about to feed her Corgis, and she wore sturdy white open-toed sandals and a cotton rose-print dress with matching Ban-Lon cardigan buttoned at the top.

I sometimes think now how surprised they must have been by my arrival. My mother had been forty-one when I'd been born, my father fifty-one. If delayed parenthood made them anxious parents, it made them no less loving or attentive. I felt their parental concern as a delicate daily web spinning around my ankles and my wrists, a web as beautiful and intricate as a spider might weave, and one that I was not at all certain I wanted to break away from.

Unlike the distracted younger parents of my classmates, mine made it clear that they expected only the best behaviour from me. Yet I knew that they would not have approved of many of my thoughts if they had known what those thoughts were: musings about ordering ten pairs of strappy leather sandals from the Eaton's catalogue, all in different shades to match my outfits, more than any of the other girls in Gilead owned. Or about discovering that I had a remarkable talent for jiving, which would make me an excellent candidate for Frosh Queen when I started Grade Nine. My parents would have been appalled that I could waste my time thinking about such trivialities. They mistook my moody silences for depth, not treacherous shallows and silliness, and I took care not to enlighten them.

I carried this knowledge as a weight in my abdomen. Sometimes when I was with them, receiving praise for a small thing I had done, such as remembering to put extra ice cubes in my father's water glass, I had the impression that I tottered on the edge of black water, and that some day I'd be pulled down into it, and no matter how much I splashed and paddled, I would sink like a block of concrete.

It was different with Mac, with his ever-judging eyes, slow to praise, so that a compliment from him about the way I swam or skied reverberated in my head for months. The summer before he'd told me that I'd developed "a truly excellent side stroke." I'd written his words down in my diary, but I knew I didn't have to do that to remember them.

The boat scraped against the dock. I grabbed onto one of the aluminum holds as Alexia approached.

"Are you going fishing?" she asked.

"Darn right." My father's voice over the hum of the engine.

"Could I ask a favour?"

"You name it."

"Could Gretchen come out with you today? I've made her lunch. She can be down here in a minute."

"Of course," my father said.

The boat could easily hold another passenger. My father

idled the engine and motioned for me to tie the painter to a cleat on the dock.

I'd asked Gretchen before if she'd like to go fishing with us. She never had.

"It's silliness, I suppose," Alexia said, as if reading my mind. "But Mac and I have to go to a meeting in Saskatoon, and I just got a call from Beryl Sullivan."

We'd met Beryl Sullivan once; she was married to Dr. Peter Sullivan, the general practitioner in Teasdale, a larger town of about three thousand people halfway between Gilead and Saskatoon.

"As I say," said Alexia, "I'm sure it's just silliness." She pushed at her French twist. "But Beryl's already seen the *Star-Phoenix* – isn't that the great thing about lake life, not having paper delivery? – and apparently they've picked up a bit about that Krywulak woman making a fuss. Beryl thinks I shouldn't leave Gretchen alone today, but it doesn't seem fair to coop her up in a car all day."

Alexia had tinted sunglasses on, the kind that hide the wearer's eyes. They made half her face appear dipped in gold leaf. She must have bought them on a trip home to Montreal; I could never find any like them, not even in the big department stores in Saskatoon.

In a way, Alexia reminded me of Jacqueline Kennedy, full of laudable childish enthusiasms and always guileless and lovely to look at. She would have been about thirty-five that summer, thin and striking. She wore a two-piece lightweight navy suit, carelessly chic, with knotty genuine leather buttons and white scalloped piping around the neck and cuffs. I couldn't remember ever seeing anyone in a suit before on the beach.

"We would absolutely love to have her," said my mother.

She turned to me, her tone as usual even and cordial and just a little reserved, much the way she might speak to the grandchildren of her friends in the United Church Women and the Icelandic Ladies Aid.

"Thora, would you mind bringing down another life jacket?"

My father's motorboat skimmed over the waves to Peter's Point with the grace of a giant motorized ballet slipper. Gretchen and I were squeezed in the bow beside him, where we had the best view of the waves. My mother rode in the stern.

A half-hearted blue tinted the sky. Clouds were building up on the western horizon. Cool lake air beat over the Plexiglas windshield and made my skin tingle.

This was a sensation I never tired of, being out on that water, unattached to anything that could hold me down. It made me feel both large and small at the same time, pressed between the sky and the water. I've been on much larger masses of water since; I've sailed the Aegean, ferried across the Bay of Biscay in January. Nothing made me feel as unfettered as I did on Whitefish Lake that summer, before everything went wrong.

My father slowed the engine as we approached Peter's Point

and eased closer to the shoreline, which was stony and
deserted, a mass of prickly brush, thistles and aspen, and a few
Javex bottles, labels long faded. I looked down over the side
and through the clear water saw smooth rocks, the flash of
minnows, and the boat's shadow, long and dark and predatory.

But when we reached the point itself, where the fishing was
usually the best, Gretchen gestured further down the shoreline to the next point.

"Have you ever been to the next bay?" she asked. "I didn't
even know there was another point beyond Peter's Point."

I thought of all the times Gretchen rode in her father's
speedboat. It seemed strange to me that she wouldn't have
noticed the other point.

My father was about to toss over the anchor.

"That one? Too many times. There's nothing much there."

"That's where Dad grew up," I said. "In a log cabin."

I'd visited the old Sigurdson homestead once, years before.
My parents had taken me when we were looking for saskatoons. The land had long since been sold to the farmer whose
cow pastures bordered most of the lake's western shore, and
from whom my father and Mac had purchased the leases to
develop West Beach. The bay in front of the old homestead
was rocky and difficult to enter and the fishing poor. No one
bothered going there.

"My dad never has time to take us sightseeing," Gretchen
said. It was a statement of fact, not a complaint.

"Perhaps he'll get a little more time now, dear," my mother
said. "With the strike and all."

"Maybe," said Gretchen.

Even now, I don't know if something in Gretchen's tone made my father feel sorry for her, or if he just wanted a change, or if he'd simply judged by the lack of other boats that the fishing wasn't going to be that good at Peter's Point that day. Or maybe he was responding to Gretchen's curiosity, a curiosity up to that day lacking in me.

"We could take a look down the lake, if you'd like," my father said.

"Absolutely," said my mother. "It's not much to see, of course."

My mother never really liked fishing, although that was something I didn't realize until much later. She only went to be with my father; by that time she'd become afraid to leave him alone for long.

I noticed none of this. I wasn't like Gretchen; I had no facility for close-hand observation.

I'd already snapped on my favourite lure, a red-and-white spoon, when my father restarted the engine. I liked the waiting part of fishing, the possibility of connecting with a living being so deep below the surface of the water you couldn't see it. The waiting part made me still inside. It seemed to make daydreaming legitimate.

"Let's take a little whirl, then," my father said. "Okay, Thora?"

"Okay."

We eased along to the next point, which was even more deserted-looking than Peter's Point, a gnarled rocky finger stabbing into the water. As we passed by, the bottom of the boat ground against a hidden rock.

"Thora," my father called, amicably. "You're supposed to warn me of those."

I looked down and saw the rock, huge and yellowish in the clear, calm water. As usual, I'd been dreaming.

We started our entry into the bay. It was easy to see why so few boats ever ventured here. Bullrushes slapped against the hull. They smelled tart and bitter, like men's aftershave.

My father turned off the engine and lifted it up so the propeller wouldn't scrape the bottom. He handed me a paddle and we gently made our way towards the shore. A rotting smell hung in the air. Masses of dead weeds clung to the beach, unlike the combed and tended sand of West Beach.

I hopped out. My feet sunk through a layer of sand to mushy, evil-smelling mud.

The others got out behind me. My mother, who loved to go barefoot, soon sank to mid-calf and laughed as mud dripped off her legs. The hooves of cattle had left squishy holes on the lake bottom. Hardened manure pies dotted the shore here and there. A barbed-wire fence, posts off kilter and only one strand left, ran down from the pasture land to the water on one side of the bay.

Gretchen ran by me, the top of her copper head barely visible above the high grass.

"Look," she said, when I caught up. She was at the base of a huge old black poplar. She reached for a sticky leaf and rubbed it against her hands.

"Dad says you can make salve from this," she said. "It's actually called Balm of Gilead. Maybe that's where Gilead got its name."

I didn't think that was how our town got its name. I was sure it was because a man named Gilead had been the first English settler. I'd read about him in one of my father's regional history books. But I didn't say anything. I liked the way small discoveries lit Gretchen's face. I felt a glow inside at the idea that my mother and my father and I could find places that would interest her, even if we couldn't offer real castles or moats or sea-battered coasts or lakes said to be inhabited by mysterious monsters.

My mother dashed back to the boat to fetch a tin can in case she saw any saskatoons.

"Isn't it way too early?" I asked, but she waved away my question in her perpetually optimistic way.

The clouds scattered like limp rags and the sun became warm, and with the warmth arose a deep rich odour, which I thought of as the sap heating up in the trees and shrubs.

"Where exactly was your father's cabin?" Gretchen asked.

"Up there, through the trees." My father pointed to a slight rise, separated from us by a reeking inlet from the lake.

"Can we go there?" Gretchen asked.

"Not much to see," my father said. He had his trousers hitched up to his knees, and the skin on his legs was creamy white, so different from his wind-reddened neck.

"It's easier by car," I told Gretchen.

One day, years before, I'd driven with my father to the

homestead along a narrow potholed road, so seldom used the municipality of Whitefish didn't even gravel it any more. I remember almost nothing about that outing. I was not a particularly curious child, certainly not about the past. For that brief time in my life, I suppose, I was like most other people. The present interested me more than the past or future.

"We could walk up there, though, couldn't we?" Gretchen said. "Just by going around there."

The route she pointed to led along the side of the marsh, above a little creek that lazily emptied into the lake. Long grasses as high as a man's head shivered slightly in the breeze.

"I'll bet that would be a good place to do a grasshopper count," Gretchen said.

"That's all for another day." My mother had caught up to us. She carried an empty tin can. Her voice had the particularly sunny lilt she assumed whenever she meant business. She slapped at a mosquito on her cheek.

And then we were back in the boat, speeding this time through the bullrushes, past Bob's Pavilion, now silent and deserted, where older teenagers went to dance and drink and neck on Saturday nights, and then back to Peter's Point where we ate egg sandwiches and fished for a couple of hours, without catching anything.

Gretchen turned to my father as we docked at West Beach later that afternoon.

"How long did you live at that cabin?" she asked.

"Until I was ten. Then we moved away from the lake."

"Why?" she asked.

"My father found some better land," he said.

"It must have been rather fun, growing up in a log cabin," she said.

My father squinted. He never wore sunglasses; all those years in cabless tractors had toughened his corneas. "Everything's fun when you're young, isn't it?" he asked.

Gretchen turned to me. "I'd like to go back there soon to do more exploring."

I wanted to return as well, although I wasn't sure why. I didn't care a whit about ancestors, or history, or pioneer life; nothing bored me more than hearing of the hardships of pioneer prairie life. I dreamed of English and Scottish queens in gold carriages or damp towers, of princesses with magic wands.

When we walked up the beach to our cabins, Rosemary and Arlene were sunning on their front lawn and reading movie magazines.

"Hey," Rosemary called out to Gretchen and me, "we're having a beach party tomorrow. You girls are invited."

"Big thrill," Gretchen said to me under her breath. She had a distracted, beneficent expression on her face that I'd seen before when she set off to gather her hoppers.

I could persuade her to come with me to the party, I realized. I'd just have to find the right way to ask.

Wednesday Evening,
JULY 4, 1962

"The eyes are the best part," my mother said. "The juiciest."

I could smell her lilac talc from where I sat, at the middle of the dining room table. The row of plate glass windows in front of me looked out on the lake.

She'd already scooped one eye out of the fish head she was eating, and was rolling it happily about in her mouth, managing at the same time to look as if she might be on her way to the Chelsea Garden Show. Her cheeks were hollowed out; she sucked as energetically at the eye as she would at hard candy.

I liked to leave the eyes for last. The trick to eating whitefish heads, it seemed to me, was selection. You had to scrape away the oily brown bits by the gill and prod with your fork for the sweet white meat along the cheeks and snout. I contemptuously flicked any dirty-looking brown meat onto my side plate, even though I knew perfectly well that some of it was tasty.

That was how Aunt Stina found us that evening, bent over our fish heads. She opened the screen door and let herself in, then dropped a few bills, along with the *Gilead Review,* the *Western Producer,* the *Free Press Prairie Farmer* and the Saskatoon *Star-Phoenix* on the table.

"Quite a lot of excitement," she said. Aunt Stina was my father's younger sister, a heavy woman with plump forearms and bright attentive eyes and a rather impassive face. On the days she went to town, my aunt collected our mail at the post office in Gilead. She and her husband Gisli also had a summer cabin on West Beach, but unlike my parents they went back and forth to Gilead every day, where they owned the hardware store and the lumberyard.

"MEDICARE EMERGENCY MOVES INTO FOURTH DAY," trumpeted the main headline in the Saskatoon paper. A subhead proclaimed, "Veterinarian's Aide Treats Mangled Leg."

I stood up so I could read over my father's shoulder. My mother rose from her side of the table. We didn't have a television out at the cabin; almost no one did.

SASKATOON – Her leg badly gashed in a waterskiing accident Tuesday, a 16-year-old teenager from Gilead, Sask., 150 miles east of here, obtained treatment from a veterinarian's assistant because the community's doctor was on strike.

Mrs. Vivienne Krywulak said she took her daughter, Rosemary, "to a chicken and horse doctor" because she knew there was no doctor at Gilead Union Hospital, twelve miles from where the accident occurred at Whitefish Lake. She said the veterinary assistant cleaned and stitched the wound.

The nearest hospital with emergency facilities is in Teasdale, seventy-five miles west of Gilead.

The incident was the first sign of citizens' growing resentment towards striking doctors in the province Tuesday, as the third day of the Saskatchewan medical strike came and went without any sign of a break in the deadlock.

The story went on to describe how Saskatchewan business was suffering from a "depression-like effect" since the weekend when the strike had started. In Regina, hospitals were operating on an emergency basis only and had been "quieter than normal."

Five British doctors had already flown over to assist the government during the crisis. One of them, Dr. Ida Cooper, had temporarily left a South London practice to be medical director of St. Anne's Hospital in Biggar, a town about the same size as Gilead.

"St. Anne's would have been forced to close if Dr. Cooper had not arrived," the story said.

The medical director of a hospital in Saskatoon was quoted as saying that four cases of coronary thrombosis were admitted within twenty-four hours after the government passed legislation guaranteeing medical insurance for all citizens.

"It may be a fluke, but we never before had that many coronary thrombosis cases admitted in such a short period," he said. "It is a scientific fact that tension aggravates the disease and it would be logical to assume that these persons were affected by the situation in this province."

One-third of the medical doctors in North Battleford who were providing emergency services planned to leave by Thursday, the story went on. No end to the political-medical dispute was in sight.

The only picture on the page showed the director of the new Medical Care Insurance Commission office in Regina issuing its first payment cheque to a doctor for patient treatment under the new Medical Care Insurance Act.

My eyes roamed the pages. The serious grasshopper outbreak was still unchecked. De Gaulle had proclaimed Algerian independence. Winston Churchill had developed "some irregularity of the pulse" while in hospital for a thigh fracture.

"Isn't that the limit?" said my mother. "As if Mac wouldn't have treated the girl if she'd just asked."

"I wouldn't be at all sure about that," Aunt Stina said. "It's a full-fledged strike. I'll bet you Mac would be in hot water with his doctor pals pretty quick if he started treating patients on his own. He's just supposed to send them to the nearest hospital that's still open."

Aunt Stina turned back to the newspaper story she was reading about the strike's effect on business.

"Gisli said he had only about a dozen customers all day," she said. "People who used to come in to the doctor's office, you see, they'd do a little shopping too."

I thought about how the fish heads were cooling. My aunt took a deep breath. She was always doing this, as if she needed the extra oxygen to move from place to place.

"Well, I guess it will end soon," she said. "Makes you a little edgy, though, doesn't it? To think there's not a hospital open for seventy-five miles. Well, I must run."

She must have only then noticed that my father hadn't said a word.

"Oh, I know," she said. "You and Mac are like that." She clamped her middle and index fingers tightly against her thumb. "Still, aren't you glad the blessed doctor wasn't on strike last March?"

As if any of us needed a reminder of when my father had suffered a heart attack.

By the time she left, a thin oily gauze had appeared over the eyes of the fish heads, and I couldn't finish them.

After supper I walked over to the McConnells'. A strong wind snapped off the water; it was a night to be indoors. It would be almost another week until Red Cross swimming lessons started. On evenings like this, the summer already seemed long.

I didn't even have to knock. Alexia saw me through the screen door.

The McConnells owned the only newly constructed cabin on West Beach, and the only two-storey structure. The interior always seemed dark to me, because of the red stain on the log walls. What Gretchen called fabric art hung on the walls and from some of the beams. These were outlines of grain fields and wheat stalks and elevators and billowing white clouds that Alexia had cut from bolts of cotton and cross-stitched into large panels. But she hadn't pieced the fabric together in the way my mother or her friends would have done, all neat and even. Alexia's stitches careened across the panels, some large, some small, and the little elevators and cut-out grain stalks tilted this way and that, as if being hurled across the prairie by tempestuous winds. Alexia called this kind of work a collage.

At the antique oak dining table, Gretchen sat gluing pictures of common garden pests into a thick scrapbook: aphids, cruciferous root beetles, imported cabbage worms, Colorado potato beetles. She looked up at me. "The organizing principle here doesn't work as well as I'd hoped," she said. "Some of the insects classified as pests actually feed on more destructive pests. It's hard to know how to label them accurately."

She shook the bottle of glue. "Science isn't as smart as science thinks," she said.

Alexia had changed into black slim jims and let down her hair, which she kept off her forehead with a hot-pink headband. She looked as if she could be Gretchen's older, more fashionable sister. I didn't see Mac, but I thought I heard voices in his upstairs study, and the faint lilt of an opera.

"Gretchen told me all about that cabin," Alexia said. "What we're thinking is, wouldn't it be fun to go on a picnic tomorrow? We could go to the old Sigurdson homestead."

I hadn't liked going to the cabin the time I'd been there with my father. The place left a lingering, restless impression on my mind of the past suspended in the present. But that night I thought of Alexia being there, with her paintbrushes and sketch pads and innocent enthusiasm, and Gretchen going off on her unpredictable ramblings, and that picture pleased me and made me feel more important than I usually did.

"Yes, let's," I said. "That sounds great."

I didn't stay long. My father wanted me to help him untangle one of the fishing nets.

But as I stepped out the door, I heard voices from above. The window to Mac's study was open. His voice was as usual clear and reassuring.

"That should fix you up just fine, laddie," he was saying. "But would you mind awfully not letting on about this? Get me in trouble with the College, you know."

"Not a word will I utter, Doc. Sure appreciate this."

A man's voice. A voice I'd heard before. A voice I should have recognized.

Wednesday,
MARCH 14, 1962

Gretchen rang the doorbell shortly after eight o'clock. This was at our new house in Gilead, the one we'd moved to from the farm the previous fall.

"Hurry," Gretchen said. "We don't want to miss seeing her open her gifts." We were on our way to a birthday party at Susan Mellers'. Susan was a girl we both liked, the daughter of the physics teacher at the high school. She'd just turned thirteen.

My mother sat at the kitchen table typing out the minutes from the Hospital Ladies Aid Auxiliary meeting. My father was at the rink, curling in the United Church Men's Bonspiel.

Gretchen wore only earmuffs on her head, and with her luminous eyes and slightly upturned nose, I thought she resembled a copper-haired elf. There were some good things about living in town, I thought. If we'd still been out on the farm, I'd never have been able to go to the party.

And then the door opened and Donald Cleland, the United Church minister, walked in. He never knocked. No one in the town expected him to any more. Members of the congregation had long gotten over their shock of being caught in dressing robes at eleven o'clock in the morning, or hair curlers at three in the afternoon.

He barely nodded to us, just walked up the stairs from the porch and stood on my mother's gleaming kitchen floor in his rubber boots.

"Jonina," he said. "I've got some bad news."

My mother rose from her typing. Ice fell in small chunks from Mr. Cleland's boots onto the linoleum.

"Better sit down," he said. He was an earnest young man, in his early thirties, who'd come out from Ontario a few years before. Gilead United Church was his first congregation.

My mother sank as if in slow motion. She didn't take her eyes off the minister.

"It's Bjorn. He's had a heart attack. At the rink."

My mother started to say something. The words garbled.

"He's at the hospital now. They're doing everything they can."

The attack occurred out on the ice, Reverend Cleland said. My father was playing third on a rink skipped by Uncle Gisli.

"Gisli had just thrown a beauty and Bjorn and the second were sweeping," said Reverend Cleland, who had organized the bonspiel and skipped his own rink.

"And then Bjorn stopped and started to complain about pains in his chest. Fortunately, Dr. McConnell was curling on the next sheet. As I say, everything that can be done is being done."

Gilead Union Hospital was only three blocks away. No one suggested we go there.

The icy chunks from the minister's boots had melted to form cookie-size pools of water on the kitchen floor.

"You'd better go alone to Susan's," I told Gretchen.

She nodded.

And then my mother and I waited together, one minute praying, then other times just sitting quietly. Mr. Cleland asked where the tea bags were and made three cups of weak Red Rose tea. He used tap water, not the special spring water my mother kept in a ceramic jug under the sink, and as a result the tea had a scum on it from all the minerals in the town's water supply.

I sat in the living room, rocking on the edge of my father's La-z-Boy, and drinking scummy tea.

It was my father's third heart attack. After the first, Mac advised him to cut down on activities. We were still on the farm then. My father did what the doctor ordered. He sold all the cattle, without much regret. The money was in wheat anyway.

The second attack came just after harvest. My father and my mother sold the farm that winter and we moved into town. Both my parents promised that town life would have many advantages over living in the country, and certainly Gilead was a pleasant and convenient community. In town, I only had to walk two blocks to the school, with its new brick gym, instead of riding on a noisy school bus for twenty minutes each way. The house my parents purchased had wall-to-wall carpeting and indoor plumbing, although my bedroom window was so high I couldn't see out unless I stood on tiptoe. A small creek ran behind the house, and this was where I spent most of my time rambling after school, wearing high rubber boots and carrying a walking stick whittled from an aspen.

Everywhere else, except for the creek and its banks, there seemed to be houses whose roofs chopped away at the sky and stole light from the windows. The farm's fifteen hundred acres seemed another world away. Later in my life, I would meet people who would express surprise that such a difference existed between farm and town life, a distance of not more than three miles. I never knew how to answer them. I only knew that the difference had to do with the way I beheld the sky in the country, open and visible to the horizon in all directions, and that part of the reason I loved Whitefish Lake was because of the way it reflected the sky and made me feel that I could fly into all that space.

I thought a lot about Gretchen and town life that night, as my mother, Reverend Cleland, and I waited to hear if my father was going to live. I wanted to think about anything except the fact that I might never see my father alive again.

Gretchen telephoned on my second endless Saturday afternoon in town. It was a blue September day.

"Would you like to come and help me today?" she'd asked. "We have a little work crew at the Rec Centre."

I didn't know Gretchen well then, although she'd been in my class for two years and the McConnells lived only a few houses down. She kept to herself. Susan, who had been to her house, said Gretchen had five science experiments underway in her basement.

"My dad says I have to do this," Gretchen said. There was no complaint in her voice, only a kind of dutifulness which later became familiar to me. "He says he can't be hounding other people to volunteer their time if his own family doesn't."

The old rink had burned down the year before. Mac had organized a steering committee to raise money and build a new one. It was supposed to be ready that winter.

We walked along a gravel road to the centre, kicking stones. I would have preferred to be on my own, climbing trees in the woods or reading one of L.M. Montgomery's *Emily* books by the creek. It occurred to me that Gretchen probably would have preferred to be in her basement working on her science projects. This realization warmed me.

When we reached the rink, which didn't have a roof yet, only four cinder block walls one storey high, Gretchen led me up a ladder to the top of the construction. The prairie rolled away, green and gold, that late September day. Here and there, sturdy lines of wind-breaking willow and caragana hedges appeared, like thick green ribbons.

The rink was being constructed in an L-shape, with one arm to be the curling rink and the other a skating rink. All afternoon we hauled cinder blocks from the middle of the floor of what was to be the curling rink. We placed them along the edge of the still-low walls, where a crew of adult volunteers lifted them and cemented them into place.

The wind blew through my hair, and for the first time since I'd moved to Gilead, I caught in it the dry, chaffy smell of grain coming off the fields, and in that scent I also caught the suggestion that I might, after all, find a way to be happy in town.

On the way home, Gretchen bought me an Orange Crush float at the Chinaman's café and asked if she could borrow *Emily of New Moon*.

"Here," she said, when I gave the book to her at the end of our outing. "Let's trade."

She slipped off the silver Celtic cross pendant she always wore and motioned to my shiny dog tag necklace which was in fashion that year, and which a great-aunt had given to me the Christmas before. I knew the Celtic pendant was worth more than the dog tag, but that didn't seem to worry Gretchen.

"There," said Gretchen, smoothing the chain of the dog tag straight on her chest. "Our friendship is sealed."

Adjusting to town life hadn't been easy for my father either. In October of that first fall after we moved to Gilead, my mother suggested that my father start hooking rugs. She picked out a pattern – a frolic of roses against a pale green background – and he began shortly after breakfast one Thursday morning.

When I came home from lunch, my father had half-finished the rug. He ate his soup with unusual haste and went back to the La-Z-Boy by the window where he began hooking again.

When I returned from school that day, the rug was completed. My father hadn't rolled it out on the floor, as I might have done, but had simply folded it into a plastic bag and left it on top of the coffee table.

He was late for supper that night.

"Where were you?" my mother asked when he arrived, shortly after seven. She'd had choir practice at seven-thirty that night and was already washing the dishes.

"Down at The Whip's," he said. The Whip was the nickname for the man who owned one of the two poolrooms on main street. I'd never been inside. It was men-only. The windows at The Whip's were streaky, and all you could see from outside were cardboard boxes piled on top of each other at odd angles and the glow of bare light bulbs.

My mother pursed her lips and wiped the last plate dry with a slow thoroughness. Then she retrieved her muskrat coat from the living-room closet and went out the door in a flash of burnished fur.

It was the first and only rug I ever saw my father hook.

But he began to be late for dinner often that fall, and sometimes he wouldn't come home for lunch either.

When he did come home he smelled of smoke and cigars.

The roof of the rink was closed in on schedule by the end of November.

One day, shortly before the new recreation centre opened, Mac called my father. It was six o'clock in the evening, and he was still at The Whip's, but I said he would return the call when he got back.

"Tell him we'll be needing a part-time caretaker for the centre," Mac said. "I was wondering if he'd be interested."

My father took the job. After that, he stopped going to The Whip's so much. He'd be at the rink early every morning, even on Sundays, flooding the ice to perfection and making sure that everything else in the building was working properly. He usually came home for supper, and when he didn't, it was because of a problem at the rink, and he always called to let us know.

Please, God, I prayed that night in March, as my mother, the minister, and I waited for news of my father. Please don't let my father die.

Of the three of us, my mother adjusted most readily to town life. Before Christmas an ad appeared in the *Gilead Review* advertising for a stenographer for the doctor's office.

My mother decided to apply. She hadn't worked in an office since before she'd married my father, thirty years earlier. But she was only fifty-four years old that summer, and I think she was beginning to see that all her time could not be filled with ladies' aid meetings and choir practices. She needed a larger ring in which to dispense her cheerfulness and good nature.

In the evenings, I would hear her typing long after I'd gone to bed. In the morning there'd be ink on her hands and under her nails from changing ribbons.

"I'm a little rusty, but I'll catch up," she'd said, gaily, digging out old steno notebooks from her days working in a Regina insurance agency. All week she practised Robertson's shorthand.

I can still see her in front of the mirror before she went for the interview. Of course she knew Mac fairly well by that time. He was a member of our church and had at one time been in the choir. All the same, my mother took extra care that morning. She flicked her dark brown hair into smooth sausage-sized rolls and blotted her lips twice, leaving tissue stained with Pond's Raspberry Rush.

"It went well," she said, when she returned from the interview.

A week later, we learned she had the job. It meant working three days a week.

My mother actually forgot one of her meetings that evening.

On that night in March, I sat on the rocker for almost an hour before the telephone rang. My mother leapt for it.

"Thank God," she said. Her voice caught. She hung up the phone and looked at me.

"He's going to be all right. We can go to the hospital now."

In a way, the McConnells had saved us all.

How much that knowledge weighed on me that long-ago

July I have been too much of a coward to try to understand. Sometimes the gratitude I knew I should feel pressed down on my shoulders like a clamp, the same way that huge sky sometimes did. Then I'd feel irritated. I'd scribble in my journal instead of playing Monopoly with Gretchen, as I'd promised, or go for long shuffling walks on the dirt road behind the cabins. Part of me sensed that some fine chain that bound me under that massive sky was loosening somewhere, but I didn't know yet where to look for the weakened link, or what I should do if I found it.

Thursday Morning,
JULY 5, 1962

"Are you sure this is the way?" Alexia asked, her voice light and silky, that of someone who expected that nothing but good could come of the day.

"Yes, I'm sure," I said. In my head I repeated my father's instructions: "Second road allowance after the turnoff to Kuroki, then the first road to the right, to a broken-down gate. Keep your eyes open. It's easy to miss."

Alexia gripped the wheel as if reining in a bronco, but she didn't brake. Wear and tear on the Buick meant nothing to her. She'd grown up in an English-speaking enclave of Montreal, a place I'd never been. A place where people drove fast and didn't worry about pedestrians, and were said to spend more on clothing than on apartments. Where the women were said to apply moisturizer before taking out the garbage. A place beyond imagining.

We'd left the main highway and the gravel secondary road and turned off on a dirt track towards the lake. Clumpy grass rose in the middle; in the tracks, dried mud had split into thick plates. On either side of the road, glossy-leafed stands of aspen shot upwards. Shrubs scraped against the car doors.

I sat beside Alexia in a low bucket seat. Gretchen was squeezed into the back, beside a picnic basket packed tight with sealer jars of strawberry Kool-Aid, egg-and-onion sandwiches wrapped in wax paper, puffed wheat cake, chocolate chip cookies, and apples. Although she'd originated the idea for the expedition, Gretchen showed little interest in the journey. She was studying a new plant identification book.

Already the air was hot, the sky hard blue tile. The car windows were closed tight because of the dust. This relieved me, since I distrusted power windows. Someone had told me about a girl in Yorkton who almost got her finger sliced off by one. My father's Pontiac was brand new; he traded his vehicle in for a new one every two years. But he never purchased any options, except for an AM radio so he could listen to the weather forecasts and the CBC crop and livestock reports from Regina.

I placed my hand for a moment on the leather-padded dash. It was soft as butter. We bumped along for about five minutes before reaching a broken-down gate.

"Turn here," I said.

Alexia swung the car into an open clearing. An old harvester, rusted to dark sienna, stood beside a log lean-to, looking like the skeleton of a long-dead beast of burden. Further on, we approached a deep, square hole in the ground, which Alexia said must be the remains of a root cellar, and then a larger, two-storey cabin, with a high, pitched roof, made of logs planed on both sides and plastered in between with a mixture of sand and lime. The buildings faced west on a plateau between two small sloping hills. The land contoured gently down to the lake, which was separated from us by a thick marsh. Beyond glimmered the bay we had explored with my parents the day before.

"So this is it?" asked Gretchen.

"What's left of it."

"And you've only been here once?"

"Yup."

"Isn't that odd?" said Alexia. "I wouldn't have been able to tear myself away. Who owns it now?"

I explained that my grandparents had sold it long ago to one of the neighbouring farmers. My grandfather had purchased a farm closer to town, with more fertile land. Only the lake and the hay meadows had attracted him here. It hadn't taken him long to realize that successful farming in this country would have to be more diverse than haying and raising sheep, which was what most farming in Iceland consisted of. When we stepped out of the car, the air smelled old and new at the same time. The scent of rotting lake weeds mingled with rust and old wood and clover and warm grass.

"Let's go in, shall we?" Alexia said. She wore white pedal-pushers that day, and sandals and a light pink percale blouse, and she didn't seem to mind that she might soil them. Even at the lake, the McConnells had an automatic washer and dryer.

I didn't like the smell of unoccupied buildings; I preferred to be outside in the light. I thought of old things as dead and useless. But the lilt in Alexia's voice pulled me.

The air in the cabin was cool. Light entered only through one window facing the lake and a few holes where the plaster had long since fallen out.

"It smells," Gretchen said.

"It's just musty," Alexia said. "You'd smell too if you were this old."

"I really want to examine the shrubbery," Gretchen said. "I'll see you guys in a few minutes." She headed for some saskatoon bushes with the plant book under her arm. I could have told her what they were if she'd asked, but she didn't.

Usually I liked to explore outdoors with her, but that morning the dim half-light inside the cabin seemed like a filmy curtain that could be tossed aside to reveal a hundred doors. Even if Gretchen didn't find the cabin interesting, I did.

"Ah," said Alexia, as our eyes began to adjust to the darkness. "You can see here, the walls used to be whitewashed."

Her long fingernails ran across the log walls. Flakes of paint were still visible by the window.

"And this must have been the cellar," she said. She pointed to a trap door in the planked floor. Boards were missing in places, so we had to tread carefully.

"I studied architecture in school, did Gretchen tell you that?" Alexia said. "At McGill. Until I met Mac. I always thought log structures deserved more respect than they got. Look at that."

She showed me how someone had tenoned a vertical post

into a horizontal sill and fitted a log into a channel in the post. *"Pièces-sur-pièces* construction," she said. "From ancient Denmark, originally. Perfect for small trees."

For a moment I thought I could picture my grandfather, axe in hand, and the sweet fresh smell of peeled bark.

"And this," I said, looking down at four deep impressions on the floor, in the form of a square. "This must have been where the stove was."

"I can just see it," said Alexia. "I bet it had six lids and a grate on one side for pots and pans. And a big reservoir for hot water."

Rickety stairs led up to the next floor. But only a few planks were left of the upstairs floor. The sky gleamed through cracks in the roof.

In the distance I heard Gretchen calling me.

"Well," said Alexia. "I think I'll go outside and do some sketching."

I hesitated on the stairs.

Alexia paused in the doorway. "If you want," she said, "we could make a miniature of the cabin for the fair. It might make a good rainy-day project. The fair's weeks away, so we'd have time."

The Gilead Agricultural Society held an annual fair in August. Alexia usually exhibited her paintings, bringing home red and blue ribbons which she stuck in unlikely places: on the bulletin board by the washing machine or tacked to a board in the potato cellar.

I thought how it would feel to construct something with

my own hands, something that was real and solid and that lasted, and I thought that was something I would never be able to do, because my thoughts always spun in so many directions at the same time. I could never seem to find the will to make them stay in one place.

"Sure," I replied to Alexia. Voice dry and flat.

Gretchen called again. I ran down the stairs. I always seemed to be going where people called me. I never had ideas of my own. I thought of myself as going through life like a tightrope walker. One step ahead was all I could think about.

But as I ran out the door into the harsh light, it occurred to me that perhaps a tightrope walker would never start out if he didn't hold, somewhere in his mind, the image of the successful last step.

"What about the Krywulaks' beach party?" I asked. We were sitting on a Hudson's Bay blanket near the cabin, drinking the last of the Kool-Aid. Alexia was already packing up the picnic basket.

"I always find it difficult to answer questions that begin with 'What about,'" Gretchen said. "What specifically are you asking me?"

"Do you want to go?"

"No," said Gretchen. She'd picked a leaf from each shrub and tree she found, and placed them in a semicircle around her: beaked willow, silver willow, green alder, hazelnut, black currant, saskatoon, hawthorn, wild rose, meadowsweet, and a few others she hadn't yet identified. "This guidebook is completely inadequate," she said. "The drawings don't show you the leaves the way the eyes really see them. They're idealized."

"It might be fun," I continued. "There'll be some kids there from Walema." That was the next big town north of Gilead on Highway 35 between Winnipeg and Saskatoon.

"You go if you want to."

"I don't want to go alone."

Gretchen rose and began to gather up the dirty paper cups and plates. If she heard me, she didn't answer. She and her parents were alike in that way. They could filter out things they didn't want to hear, things that were inconvenient or unpleasant or went against what they thought should be spoken or done. I didn't know how to be like that, and I hadn't yet learned how useful such an ability could be.

"Grab one end, will you?" Alexia asked. She'd picked up two corners of the blanket and motioned me to help her.

"Beach parties are fun, aren't they?" she said. "I don't blame you for wanting to go."

"Even if it's at the Krywulaks', Mom?" Gretchen asked.

"Oh well," Alexia shrugged. She looked as if she might say something else, but she didn't, she just shook the blanket so vigorously she almost pulled it out of my hands.

Before we left the homestead, I approached the cabin one more time, and ran my hand along the door frame. It was low. Alexia, who was of medium height, had to bend down to enter.

The darkness inside tugged at my chest. The breeze had dropped. Even the aspens had stopped trembling.

Inside the car, the air smelled of insecticide and sweat. The red vinyl burned against my damp flesh.

Gretchen propped her plant book on her knees, trying to identify the remaining leaves.

On the drive back, a funny thing happened. I started building pictures in my head. The pictures were all of the log cabin, but not the way it looked that day. Instead, I tried to picture the interior as it might have been when people lived there: perhaps with a table, three or four chairs, a few hand-carved chests. It was as though the air I breathed had transformed itself into layers of time. If I thought hard enough and breathed deeply enough, I thought I might be able to squeeze myself back into those spaces in time. And none of the people I would meet back then would be threatening or want anything from me or have the ability to disappoint; all I would ask of them was their acquaintance.

The Buick seemed to ease itself over the worst sections of the back road with more grace than it had during our approach. When we reached the highway, Alexia switched on the radio. It was just after three o'clock, so we caught the first news item.

"The provincial medical dispute appears to have claimed its first casualty," announced an excited voice. "A nine-month-old baby from Newbridge died on the way to Yorkton Union Hospital last night. The cause of death is believed to be meningitis.

"Alexander Cawsey was taken to Yorkton yesterday by his parents by car," the announcer continued. "During the day they noticed the baby was sick, and they tried to obtain medical advice by telephone from the local hospital in Newbridge. They were told the doctor was not available and were advised to go to the Yorkton emergency centre.

"The boy's father, Edward Cawsey, told CKQT he would like to know how Premier Lloyd is going to compensate him for a thing like this. Newbridge is forty miles south of Yorkton."

The road curved west, into the sun. "Hand me my sunglasses, will you?" said Alexia. "They're in the glove compartment."

I wanted her to turn off the radio.

The announcer continued, his tone neutral. A mass rally was being organized at the legislative grounds in Regina for the following Thursday, he said. The organizers were "the militantly anti-government Keep Our Doctors Committee."

The news ended with Premier Lloyd saying that such mass meetings should be "restrained and prevented."

I turned to Gretchen. Her head was bent over her book.

Alexia switched stations and sang "I Can't Stop Loving You" along with Ray Charles.

Friday Afternoon,
JUNE 19, 1998

The entrance to the Provincial Museum of Northern Alberta is full of shrieking school children, here to see the Bats exhibit. The breeze carries the scent of lilacs and the air is warm. On the car radio, the CBC announcers are predicting a fine weekend for camping. I expect to spend most of Saturday and Sunday burrowed in my office in the basement of the museum.

I manoeuvre my way around a group of high school students. "Well, pardon me," a teenage girl with frizzy brown hair says as I slip by, although she's barely left me space to squeeze past.

"At least she's here," I can almost hear my boss, Ches Longman, saying.

My Birkenstocks click along the linoleum stairs. Lorraine, the secretary for our section, says she knows when I'm approaching. "You always sound as if you know exactly where you're going," she says.

This makes me feel happy and hopeless at the same time,

because if I know at all where I'm going it's because of Gretchen. The influence of my work, of course, must also be acknowledged. In my field, historical archaeology, my job is to look backward and at the same time figure out what the future would have looked like from an earlier perspective. Some of my colleagues think my job is easier than theirs – I deal with the period of Western Canadian history after the written word appeared, with a particular interest in turn-of-the-century Scandinavian settlement. Unlike archaeologists who specialize in earlier times in Western Canada, I have more than fire circles and projectile points to work with. More than the pure historians too, confined as they seem to be by the written word.

I pity them, really. They don't have the archaeologist's sense of how much you can tell about people from things. Just holding the brass hairbrush owned by the chief factor's daughter at Fort Sunwapta told me more about how she viewed the world than any of her tedious little journals, with their ridiculous summaries of dinner menus and the progress of her bronchial disease.

That hairbrush, and her shell buttons, specially ordered from London, suggested how superior she felt compared to almost everyone else at the fort. Whereas the artifacts that Markus Olafsson left reveal him as a man of truly democratic impulses, whose life entirely paralleled his belief in independence, self-improvement, and progress as the path to salvation. His material possessions, especially the marvellous site he chose for his homestead, are entirely compatible with his written record.

The Site Restoration Section at the museum is cramped, just two chairs in a waiting area, a central desk for Lorraine, and two adjoining offices: one for Mike Radwell, who's in charge of the prehistoric archaeological sites for the division, and mine. The brass nameplate on my door says "Thora Sigurdson, Restoration Manager, Alberta Historic Sites." A large smudge appears between my first and last name. I never noticed it until today. I polish the plate quickly with a tissue. Keeping a shine on one's exterior surroundings discourages dust from settling on the brain cells, Markus joked in his letters. This is definitely not a time for me to have dust settling on mine.

My thoughts always seem to be flitting back to Markus's time. It's not exactly an accident. I've trained myself not to get mired down in the present. Actually, I do my best to ignore the present, except as it relates to the work at hand. That's what wore Paul down so much.

Delete those "Paul" thoughts, I chide myself. I'm acting like a schoolgirl instead of a forty-nine-year-old.

That's easier to do when I reach the end of the hall. On entering my office, a visitor would, I believe, be struck by an impression of quiet competence. I'm snug and content and in control here, small though my quarters are. The surface of my desk is clear, except for one letter and a neat pile of a hundred and twenty invitations to the July 1 opening, which I'll have Lorraine mail on Monday. The posters for the new carriage museum and automobile museum, recently mounted in brass frames, gleam pleasingly on either side of the long, narrow window that looks out on the parking lot. Today it's full of school buses.

The letter is an invitation to a staff barbecue for the entire department. I drop it into the wastebasket and I dial Kramer in maintenance. He says he's stopped the leak but will keep checking on it.

"Where's it coming from?" I ask. "We had new rain gutters and downspouts put in."

I'd approved all the standard drainage practices during the new construction phase. We hadn't allotted any money for rebuilding the somewhat crumbling foundation, but we'd had an engineering firm reinforce the structure with a few steel beams and posts. Naturally, I tried to toe the line on extra expenditures. Another fifty thousand in the budget and we might not have gotten the restoration approved in the first place.

"Could be a lot of places," says Kramer.

"I'm just worried about what could happen over the weekend."

"Don't worry," he says. "I'll have another look last thing today."

I answer with silence, a technique I find extremely useful. I imagine a hint of a smile on Kramer's bland, good-natured face. He's nearly sixty and has worked for the maintenance department for thirty years, I'd guess. He's a balding, unremarkable man, reliable enough but with just a touch of insolence that irritates me, and that he cannot be unaware of.

"Well, okay," Kramer adds. "I'll look in over the weekend too."

I'm awash in paperwork when Svava Erlendson, the president of the Friends of the Markus Olafsson Site Society, floats into my office without an appointment. She doesn't so much sit down on a chair in my office as appear to crush it, her doughy arms rolling over the slim armrests. Like many seriously overweight women, her complexion is as fresh and lovely as a young girl's. Her brown eyes shine with a victor's joy.

She kicks off her sandals. "It's just too good to be true," she says. "We did it! Jon Arnesson is confirmed for the opening!"

"Wait, wait," I say, trying to slow her down. The dream of historical archaeologists is to have spirited and committed volunteers support their pet projects, but sometimes I wish Svava didn't burn on such high gas. She's been trying for months to have the new Icelandic-Canadian Consul, Jon Arnesson, who is based in Winnipeg, present at the opening. She's also making a last-ditch effort to have The Snowlands Choir from Iceland perform at the opening. The choir is touring in Eastern Canada and Manitoba this month, so it might be able to extend its tour further west. In addition, there's a possibility of starting a Markus Olafsson Scholarship fund for young Alberta "West Icelanders."

"That would be a coup," I tell Svava.

She nods brightly. Like me, she's well aware that visits by Icelandic dignitaries are rare in Alberta, which has a small population of Icelandic-Canadians. The majority live in Manitoba.

"Where's the funding coming from?" I ask.

Svava names a local businessman, someone of Icelandic descent who is donating the funding in memory of his father.

"It was the Olafsson house that got the donor interested," she says. "He said, and I quote: 'If the Icelanders in Alberta pull off something like that, I've enough confidence to fund the scholarships.'"

"That's great."

She gives me a quizzical look.

"Are you okay? You seem a little down."

For a moment, it occurs to me to tell her about the seepage, but I catch myself in time.

"Just tired."

After Svava leaves, I turn to my computerized "to-do" list. There's an e-mail from Longman that I should respond to. He's the division director, well into his sixties, a rather stern but conscientious bureaucrat who's been here since the free-spending days of the oil boom. Now he watches over public expenditures like a hungry hawk over a hay meadow. We actually did receive a memo not long ago asking that staff take care to recycle office supplies, including paper clips, whenever possible.

"Just checking on how plans are proceeding for the opening," he's written. "Imperative that parking arrangements be in place for VIPs. Also, one of the MLAs is querying costs in Question Period and we'll need to do a briefing note for the Minister. Will definitely need to keep the lid on."

"Will have blacktop in by next week," I respond. "Okay re: budget. I'll draft a briefing. May have some small groundwater problems but being attended to."

After I hit "send" on that message I notice that another e-mail has come in. The name on the inbox brings a flush to my cheeks.

Paul Merrill, the geologist I lived with until recently. He's left several telephone messages since he moved out three weeks ago.

For a moment I consider deleting the message without reading it, but I can't make my finger hit the key. Instead I ignore the message and try to go on to the next task.

Damn Paul, anyway.

Funny, how quietly our relationship ended. A few weeks ago, we took a long walk after work, as we usually did. Like most geologists, Paul is never happier than when he is outdoors, and on that day we walked through Dawson Park, where he took some photos of the hoodoos. In his spare time, when he's not consulting for large oil and gas companies, Paul is working on a geological history of Edmonton.

He was particularly pleased that day, because he had obtained a rare photograph of one of the first coal mines in the river valley. He'd uncovered it the previous evening when he visited an aged civil engineer, now living in a nursing home, who had worked in the mine as a boy. "There's so much more here than you'd ever think, from the surface," he said that day. "Old coal mines, mastodon bones, even."

We were crossing the Capilano Bridge, and paused for a moment to look down at the river. I quoted a few lines roughly translated from Markus's poem, "North Saskatchewan in Flood."

All day I walk alone with you,
Threading the valley to the river's secret bend.

I see your depths and shallows,
And the distant blue pillars you called home.

Paul turned to me, with a questioning look on his face, and I was struck again by how youthful he is for his fifty-two years. He's a big man with a long, thin face, a neat grey ponytail and deep brown eyes. They seem to warm at everything he looks at: his work as a geologist, his clients, his mailman. I wouldn't be surprised if he had good words to say about Revenue Canada.

"You never talk about your childhood," he said. "What kind of kid you were, who your friends were, almost nothing."

"There's not much to tell," I lied.

For a moment Paul looked as if I'd given him an invisible slap. "Never mind," he said.

Later that evening, he asked to see my childhood photo albums. He knew where I kept them, in a cupboard in the room he used as a study. The room wasn't large, so I'd cleared half of the cupboard for him to store some of his overflowing research papers.

"I'm not ready," I said.

"Ready for what?"

"Ready to show you those pictures."

"I don't care if you had pimples then, for Christ's sake."

"It's not that."

"Then what is it?"

I didn't answer. That must have been the evening he began packing, at least in his head.

We're a month behind where we should be with the interpretive display on Markus's life that will be presented in conjunction with the opening. Carrie Nelson, the thirtysomething in-house designer, gave me the same answer all spring whenever I asked how the panels were coming along: "You haven't given me enough material!"

"I don't want to overburden you," I told her. "I want to keep it simple, just enough to whet people's interest. A few strong graphics, some bits from his poetry."

"That's not the way I prefer to work," she'd said. "I like to start with the whole story and whittle it down."

"Try my way, " I suggested. I deliberately didn't provide her with a copy of the chapter written on Markus's life in *Notable Icelandic-Canadians,* by the Icelandic-Canadian scholar, Ena Ericson. I didn't want Carrie to get too bogged down with details.

My face burns a little at that memory. Jesus. Carrie's only been here for six months. I should take it easy on her. Is it true what Paul said, that this project is bringing out the Viking in me, and it's not a pretty sight?

Thora, Thora. Soon I'll be seeking out human sacrifices.

I'm filled with a mixture of anticipation and anxiety as I unroll the mock-up Carrie left on my desk the night before. The headline that extends over all three panels is catchy enough: It calls Markus "The Rebellious Rocky Mountain Poet of Alberta."

The panels describe his early works, his many Rocky Mountain poems, his middle period when he wrote *Harvest* and *Glacier Streams* and excerpts from the first two volumes of *Sagas of the West Icelanders*. Carrie's followed my suggestion, glossing over the silent last years, and simply stated that Markus "disappeared on September 21, 1920, and although his body was never recovered, he is believed to have drowned in the North Saskatchewan River."

The panels seem fine in themselves, but incomplete. I instructed Carrie not to devote much space to the story of Markus's immigration to Canada from Iceland, or to portray much about Icelandic culture. Keep it simple, I kept reiterating.

"You mean, dumb it down?" she asked.

"No, that's not what I mean at all," I'd said. "It's just that people won't take much time to look at the panels anyway. We only have time to hit them with a few facts about Markus's life."

Carrie says the panels need final copy approval by Tuesday so the display can be mounted. I'll mull them over on the weekend.

Silly of me, I suppose, to think I'd be the one to answer a question that has puzzled literary scholars all this time. Working with the physical realities of Markus's life (the posts and beams of his house, the metal turn buttons for the storm windows, the shiplap spruce siding) would give me an advantage in uncovering the mysteries surrounding Markus, I reasoned, because I would be able to picture better than anyone else the material confines of his world. The physical remains of the past don't tell lies or skirt around reality the way the written word can. And although these physical remains leave gaps, they can also leave clues.

What faith I place in the patient slogging of my discipline! And, at times, how bountifully my faith has been repaid. I was still an undergraduate that summer in 1973 when I worked with Dr. Iswold at Fort McGregor in northeast Alberta. For weeks we sifted through mud chinks, glass fragments, cellar depressions and chips of wood, trying to find some clues to life in the North West Company fort, which we knew had once stood there but which had burned down in the nineteenth century.

"Here are our answers," Dr. Iswold said one day during our fifth week in the field. He was nearing seventy by then, still nervous with energy, bony fingers outstretched. He pointed to the piles of fired mud chinking we'd unearthed in the south quadrant. I shook my head when he said he was going to have the chinks boxed and sent to the lab in Edmonton.

In the end, we recovered eighty-five boxes of chinking from every quadrant of the site. What we found formed the basis of my doctoral thesis. The negative impressions in the mud were as clear as a social register in the information they yielded about the status of various buildings on the site, and therefore of the residents. How crude the chinking on the barracks buildings! How lacking in craft! And how carefully wrought the chinking on the chief factor's quarters!

As I look more closely at the interpretive panels Carrie provided, I'm more aware than ever of how much is missing. There are so many other questions that must be posed about Markus's life, questions I'd hoped I'd be able to answer by now.

How can his disappearance be explained? And why did he

stop writing for his last six years?

The historical record, which tells us so little about most of Markus's life, seems clear enough on a few points: he quit writing poetry entirely in 1914, although he was only sixty-one years old, presumably at the peak of his powers, and had only one more volume of poetry to write to complete his trilogy, *Sagas of the West Icelanders,* which many critics think would have unquestionably sealed his reputation as the pre-eminent Icelandic poet of all time. Yet for forty-one years previously, he wrote prodigiously, sometimes a poem a day.

During this long, last silence, Markus's writings consist only of his journals and his correspondence. Voluminous as they are, they give few hints of his reasons for deserting the muse. They do suggest that he enjoyed good health during this period, as he did all his life, and that the difficulties he faced on the homestead were no more or less than he faced during productive times. But except for the briefest mention, his correspondence and journals are almost entirely lacking in personal content. He mentions his wife, Helga, only occasionally, and then usually in association with a chore that she is completing or news she has received from relatives in Iceland or the Dakotas. It's as if he funnelled all his joy for life into his poetry, and after the hard work the homestead required, he didn't have the energy to record what he must have considered the mundane details of daily life.

His love for his Alberta homestead is unquestioned, which presents the other puzzle. Why did he leave it that late summer day in September, 1920, and simply disappear? At least a few of Helga's letters survive. She says her husband had been in vigorous good spirits that month, pleased with the hay crop, and at work on what she believed was the third volume of *Sagas of the West Icelanders.* Of course, no fragment has ever been found of such a manuscript. "I happened to see him walking towards the river, just before supper on the day of September 21, 1920," she wrote her sister, Begga, in Winnipeg. "I thought he'd gone to check on the river levels – it had been raining for three days. But he never returned."

There are no suggestions that Markus had been experiencing depression, no signs of a let-up in energy. He'd continued to work the farm as industriously as ever, and had planned a trip to an Icelandic gathering in Wynyard, Saskatchewan, that fall to read his poetry.

Oh, I know the usual reasons given to explain the apparent extinction of Markus's creative life, but I don't find them adequate. We know from Helga's correspondence that Markus grieved deeply for his second eldest son, Siggi, who had been struck by lightning in a hayfield in August, 1914, at the age of eighteen. Yet there is no reason to believe that Siggi's death alone would have caused Markus to stop writing. He'd already lost his eldest son, Einar, to diphteria two years before, without any sign of a reduction in his creative output. Nor could the beginning of World War I be a satisfactory explanation, although Markus was a zealous pacifist who actively resisted the war and encouraged others to do so. If anything, we could have expected the war to increase his output. Helga recalls him vowing on the day that war was declared that he would "continue to fight the war with words, which are my only artillery."

It's getting late, and my shoulders ache. From the stillness in the corridor, most of my colleagues seem to have left for the day. I go to a bookshelf, take down *Notable Icelandic-Canadians,* then walk down the hall to copy the chapter on Markus's life from Ericson's history. I stick the copied pages into a manila envelope. Carrie lives in an apartment just off Whyte Avenue. I'll drop it off on the way home. She said she'd appreciate anything more that could help make Icelandic life and beliefs more real to her.

Then I roll up the panels. I'm aware of a little glow of pride within me. Sure, there are still questions to answer, and the omissions trouble me. Yet we know so much more about Markus's life than we did before we started the restoration, and the farmstead will keep yielding clues. I'm absolutely confident about that. Sticks and stones can tell you things the past would otherwise hide. This is the promise that keeps me riveted to my field, the promise that will help me make my amends to Gretchen.

I'm still buoyant with that thought when I return to my e-mail and open the message from Paul. He's invited me to dinner on Saturday night.

I read the message one more time. Then, perhaps because I've been thinking about Gretchen more often than I usually do, I recall the advice she used to give me when I was afraid to dive into the lake.

"Just plunge in," she'd say. "Just plunge. It's the only way."

"Fine," I e-mail back to Paul. "See you at seven tomorrow."

Thursday Afternoon,
JULY 5, 1962

Rosemary lay on her back on the low diving board, her arms dangling in supplication to the sun. I could barely discern a patch of white on one leg: she was still bandaged from the accident. Arlene reclined on her stomach on the platform of the raft, head on her elbows. Both of them inert as stone. The little rowboat provided by the rental cabin bobbed on its line.

I watched them through binoculars after Alexia dropped me off at my parents' cabin. The air held the sweet summer scent of cut grass. The lake itself glowed like mercury. Smoke from forest fires had drifted south and softened the day's sharp edges. Except for two toddlers at the water's edge with their mother, there was nobody on the beach.

Since entering the cabin at the Sigurdson homestead earlier that day, I'd experienced an extraordinary sensation of alertness. I felt nervy and aglow. An urge came over me to try a swan dive off the low board, which I'd never done before.

I stripped in the small changing room at one end of the

bunk room and reached for the bathing suit hanging from a nail. The suit was a pink two-piece with spaghetti straps and frills along the waist and bodice. I had no bust to speak of, so the effect was little more flattering than having pink tape wrapped around my chest. This did not bother me in the least. My reasons for wanting a two-piece were much more practical: comfort. A two-piece didn't keep your stomach soggy when you lay on the beach suntanning; and it wasn't so likely to catch on the slivery bits of wood on planked piers.

In the water, I did a duck dive and headed directly for the raft. The distance between the shore and the raft seemed shorter than the few other times I'd swum there alone.

When I reached the raft, Rosemary was still dozing on the end of the diving board. She and Arlene reminded me of minor European princesses that day, suntanned and faintly elegant, with big rings on their carefully manicured fingers. I recognized the rings from the Robinson's store. You could buy them for a few dollars.

I climbed up. Water dripped at my feet. I yearned for the sensation of springing into the air, knowing that in a few seconds I'd be embraced by cool water.

"Hi, cutie-pie," said Rosemary, in a not-unfriendly tone. She turned over on her stomach and took off her sunglasses. Their lime-green plastic frames seemed to frown and I braced myself for some unknown obstacle. Rosemary made no further attempt to move. She wore a pale blue one-piece shirred nylon suit fitted with foam-rubber bra cups that pushed her breasts together, so you could see the cleft between them. Her skin gleamed with Johnson's baby oil. The cloying scent hovered over the raft. The tiny charms on her bracelet made dancing shadows against the canvas of the diving board. Part of me felt honoured that she'd acknowledged my presence.

"I like your suit," she said. "You're lucky. You're slim. A perfect parfait."

I wondered if she was making fun of me. I had no idea what a perfect parfait was.

"Now me," she said. "The goblet shape was invented for the likes of me." She was sitting up now, and had stretched her short legs in front of her on the board. Close up I could see that the bandage on her right leg was stained with grit and baby oil.

"So, anyway," she said. "You coming to the beach party?"

I said I didn't know. I was getting cold just standing there, but I didn't want to sit down. I worked at willing her to move off the diving board without having to ask.

"How's your leg?"

"It'll be okay," she said. "I just can't get it wet for ten days. That's why I rowed out."

"I'm really sorry."

"Don't have a bird. It was an accident. By the way, where's your friend?"

"Pardon?"

"Your friend. Gretchen."

"I don't know," I said. It occurred to me that Rosemary saw Gretchen's shadow every time she looked at me. The thought irritated me, like a pebble in a running shoe.

I knew perfectly well that Gretchen had gone back to her room to press her new leaf specimens. This, I imagined, would amuse Rosemary, who seemed to be waiting for me to say more. The thought of her laughing at Gretchen was more than I could stand, even though I knew it wouldn't really be a cruel laugh, just light and careless.

"She's not that big on swimming," I explained.

Rosemary still showed no sign of moving, although I obviously wanted to use the board. Arlene hadn't budged either, or uttered a word since I'd arrived, but as usual I had the impression that she was watching and listening, and that she didn't miss much that went on.

"So," Rosemary said. That was the way she always seemed to preface her sentences. "So." As if everything was predetermined.

"Your parents going to that rally in Regina next week?"

"I don't know," I answered, truthfully.

"I should imagine," Rosemary said. "Your parents being so close to the doc and all."

"I really haven't the faintest idea." My voice a lake weed, drifting.

Clearly Rosemary wasn't going to move, and I was too timid to ask. I backed off and approached the ladder to the high diving board. Never before had I thought of diving off that board; it was really only for older kids, sixteen or seventeen, kids who had attained their Seniors' badges in Red Cross swimming lessons. Some parents thought the high board should be dismantled. They said it encouraged teenagers to try foolish stunts. Mac disagreed. He told Gretchen and me that it was important to know your limits and that you couldn't know them without testing them.

I started climbing, on automatic pilot, responding to some mysterious invisible signals emitted by the smoky light and the sheen of the grey water.

The high board didn't have as much flex as the low board. I walked to the edge. Just jump, I told myself. I leapt into the air and bounced once off the board. As my feet left the board the second time my arms arched above my head and my back curved and I was diving down into the water fifteen feet below.

I glided deep under the surface. The water a hazy greyish green. Cold and reassuring. Part of me didn't want to ever go up for air; for a moment everything seemed safe and simple.

When I did surface, I realized my error. I hadn't thought about how the high board was placed at an angle veering towards the middle of the lake, far beyond my normal swimming limits. Here the water was way over my head.

I hadn't thought about anything, really.

I wanted to get back to shore as soon as I could. For a moment I treaded water. My fingers felt numb. From down the beach I heard the distant hum of a motorboat. I didn't think the Krywulak twins would be watching, but as I gazed at the beach, the realization came into my head that Mac might be able to see me. I imagined him on the upper balcony adjacent to his study, in bermuda shorts and with a lemonade glass at his side, listening to *The Tales of Hoffman* or another one of his beloved French operas, and observing me bob clumsily in the water, like a confused gull. The thought made me shrink and at the same time puffed me up. Before my mind could clamp down on my actions, I was swimming further out towards the middle of the lake. Further than I'd seen anyone except Mac swim without a boat behind for safety. My blood vessels throbbed and amplified, heating my inner core. I only turned back when my body, not my head, told me it was time.

Stepping out of the water that afternoon, I felt cleaner than I had ever felt before. As if my insides had been scrubbed by ice cubes. I felt stronger, too. I suppose some people would call this confidence, but now I'm not sure. Whatever you want to call that feeling, it wasn't always there when I needed it that summer.

Thursday Evening,
JULY 5, 1962

My father worked faster than Uncle Gisli; he had been doing this since he was six. First he placed the three pickerel on their sides. Then he cut behind each head. The filleting knife slid softly through the skin, as if through grapefruit, down to the backbone. Swiftly he ran the knife along the spine. Straight hard cuts. Silver-white scales oozed onto the pier.

The two men toiled in unison, not seeming to notice for a moment my footsteps or my shadow above them. My father turned the fish over, slit the white belly from the vent to the throat. Then he jogged the knife to get the fin out of the way before the final skinning: a little trick he'd taught me too, even though I didn't like to fillet fish and have never enjoyed handling dead things.

I'd changed after my swim into shorts and a kangaroo top, and walked down to the dock when I saw my father's boat approach. Back in the cabin, my mother peeled sprouty potatoes from last year's garden. She didn't ask me to help. She told me often enough that childhood is for pleasure. At times this made me anxious: what was adulthood for, then?

"I figure we need to show our support," Uncle Gisli said. He was watching my father.

"Maybe, maybe," my father said. He paused to spit some chewing tobacco into the lake. It bobbed on the surface like a brown cork.

"That Krywulak incident got people worked up," Uncle Gisli continued. He was a small man, tidy and careful. For several years he had been the mayor of Gilead, until he found out he had diabetes and had to slow down.

"You'd think they'd know better," said my father. I recognized the tone as one he often directed at me. The one that said he always expected logic of others.

"And then that baby dying down in Newbridge," Uncle Gisli said. "Everyone's blaming the doctors, when it's the government's fault for trying to get away with this. We let the politicians tell the doctors how to run their business, and the next thing you know they'll be telling me how to run my business. Or farmers, for that matter. They won't be happy until they make Ruskies out of all of us."

My father sliced the last fillet and put it into the ice bucket, then began to wrap the fish tails in old newspapers.

"I'm just saying," said Gisli, "attending that Regina rally is the least we can do. If there are enough people, it'll make them think twice."

"Thora," said my father, who had at last noticed I was there. "Give the dock a little scrub, will you?"

The idea of being useful emboldened me.

"You know," I said, "this was probably all my fault. If I hadn't hurt Rosemary Krywulak that day skiing, people wouldn't be so mad at Mac."

Uncle Gisli looked at me curiously and began to laugh. So did my father.

"My girl, my girl," Uncle Gisli said. "People like the Krywulaks always find something to bleat about. Don't worry about the dock. I'll scrub it clean as a whistle in a jiffy."

I sauntered back up to the cabin and leafed through a *Redbook* article about choosing the correct swimming suit for your figure. "If you're a perfect parfait," the article said, "you can wear anything."

A perfect parfait, according to the writer, occurred when bust and hips were both ten inches larger than the waist.

My face felt hot. A perfect parfait, indeed.

I looked at my bathing suit, a wet pink ball on the linoleum floor, and I could see then that it was all wrong for me, that it exposed the thinness of my ribs and hips and the flatness of my chest, which looked like a boy's. Bathing suits weren't just for swimming. My face felt warm. At the same time I was oddly excited, as if those bits of fabric had all along held more power than I'd given them credit for.

I glanced around the bunk room I shared with my parents, the life jackets hanging from nails by the high window, the scratched two-drawer walnut chest, the faded linoleum floor with its pattern of swirling green leaves. How meagre it all seemed, how lacking in dash.

Could I have been wrong all this time in the way I looked at things? How stupid I was, only to scan the surfaces.

Friday Morning,
JULY 6, 1962

Gretchen and I running fast, down the dirt road behind the cabins, past the confectionery stand with its coat of fresh paint, across the gravel road, along an abandoned mud track bordered by a broken-down barbed-wire fence. Summerfallow on the other side. Gretchen keeping ahead, even though she's carrying the sweeping net, her copper hair flying, canvas running shoes thudding against hard-baked earth. Pink-cheeked, giggling and bursting ahead each time I almost catch up. The lake a smooth blue sheet. The sun warm. The scent of alfalfa in the rain-rinsed air.

Gretchen struck people as a well-behaved, serious girl, objective in the way adolescents rarely are, and it's true that she was all these things. In our school she was liked well enough by our classmates; she'd never hesitate to take notes for a student who was sick or even correct a teacher on a small point; these were all things she did modestly, with good cheer. But she possessed other qualities that most overlooked. This is what I have told myself in the intervening years, although the truth is that I don't quite believe it myself. Only once in a while, in the summer usually, on days like that day, my mind catches a thin thread and tries, never successfully, to pull it in before the connection snaps.

I can see Gretchen standing where the summerfallow gave way to a hay meadow. "Shhhhh," she said. Fingers to lips.

We crossed under the barbed-wire fence. As we stepped into the meadow, blades of grass tickled our knees. Everywhere we walked, grasshoppers jumped. They were the most tender shade of green, and small. They reminded me of demented jelly beans. The hay smelled sweet and wild.

Gretchen brought the killing jar out of her knapsack. It was just a mayonnaise jar, with a lid that closed tightly. She'd already placed a lump of plaster of Paris, soaked with nail polish remover, at the bottom. She began to move the net back and forth rapidly through the grass. Even in performing such a simple act, Gretchen moved with the utmost dignity. The dog chain around her neck swung back and forth on her chest. In her brown eyes, I caught a look of concentrated stillness.

"There," she said. "Hold the jar on the ground. Steady."

She grabbed the net below the rim and twisted it tight. At the bottom of the net, dozens of grasshoppers jumped. She shook the insects into the bottom of the jar, withdrew the net, and quickly put the top back on.

"This will only take a few minutes," she said.

We watched intently. I could hear the hoppers rustling in the jar. Gradually the sounds stopped. Gretchen nodded, confirming the death of the hoppers. All around us, other more fortunate hoppers leaped about.

My knees hurt, and the back of my throat felt raw and dry. My mind flashed to how cool it had been inside the old Sigurdson homestead, and how dark, and how I hadn't minded the spider webs and the greasy floors. All that darkness and decline seemed to me to hold the promise that more could be found there than one might expect, not like the scene before me now, with the terrible clarity of the morning light casting shadows with edges as sharp as knives.

"There," said Gretchen. She frowned as she looked into the jar. "These look like immatures. I'll weigh them when I get home. Then you can help me double-check them tomorrow."

"Okay."

I'd agreed to help Gretchen examine the hoppers and separate the nymphs from the matures. This wasn't too difficult to do with dead hoppers, although it took time. Sometimes Gretchen kept the hoppers alive under observation for a few weeks, and then we'd have the laborious but important task of separating them all beforehand. If we didn't do this, Gretchen said, cannibalism could become a serious problem. For a reason not understood, the mature hoppers in confinement sometimes launched frenzied feeding attacks on young females.

I didn't like looking at the hoppers in the jar. I liked to see them sprint above the grass, with leaps high and wild and a little crazed.

We walked back to the lake. I thought about how some hoppers had been lucky that morning, and some unlucky, and how the lucky ones wouldn't even realize how fortunate they'd been.

When we parted for lunch that day, I asked Gretchen, "If I keep on helping with the hoppers, will you come with me to the party?"

It was hotter now, the sun above our heads and the air still. I could tell Gretchen had been hoping that I'd forget about the party. She looked down at the killing jar she held in both hands, fingers laced around the glass. I had the impression of compressed energy, like a young hurricane.

"All right," she said, a tinny sound in her voice. "As long as we only stay for a little while."

Friday Evening,
JULY 6, 1962

Flames from the driftwood fire licked high above my head, crackling like small whips.

A transistor radio, turned to high volume, blared out "Sweet Little Sheila" from a Regina rock 'n' roll station. The same lilt of carefree summery joy in the song could be heard in the voices all around me. Rosemary and Arlene had dragged in railway ties to form a large circle around the fire, but almost everyone stood or shuffled about in the sand. I recognized a few people, all high school students several years older than Gretchen and me. There were a lot I didn't know, kids from other towns, I assumed, or kids whose parents had cabins across the lake at Walema Beach. They roasted marshmallows and drank beer and sang along to the radio in an off-key, good-natured manner; a few couples pressed close to each other at the far edges of the fire.

"Name your poison!" said Rosemary.

She appeared before us, ponytail swinging. She had on a black T-shirt and tight blue cut-offs that showed her midriff, and nothing on her feet. The bandage on her right leg had been freshly changed.

It was starting to occur to me that Rosemary had what the American magazines for teenagers called "flair." Flair was something you either had or did not have. It was much more desirable to have flair than not have flair. But if you didn't have flair, you could concentrate on your other strengths. Some of those other strengths could be neatness, cleanliness, or cheerfulness.

I was sure I could never be neat; every time I breathed, grit accumulated under my fingernails. But I could at least be cheerful. I did my best to smile brightly at Rosemary, and hoped I didn't look all teeth, like the lady in the Dentine commercial.

At the same time, I felt a shudder of gratitude towards Gretchen for being there. Together, we could blend into the background of the beach party. If we didn't succeed, we could at least prop each other up.

"Beer, rum? Mix?"

Rosemary's voice lifted at the end of the sentence. She dug her feet into the sand. How easy it would be for her to step on a burning coal. Gretchen and I wore matching pedal-pushers and tops made of polished cotton and canvas running shoes.

Someone turned up the volume on the transistor. Dean Martin's voice drifted lazily into the sky.

"I'll just have some mix, thanks," said Gretchen.

"Same for me."

"All right, girls," Rosemary said. She brought back plastic

tumblers filled with Seven-Up. "Now go ahead, mingle."

I could tell she didn't want to stay with us, and she quickly moved away. I wondered why we'd been invited.

We started to circle the edge of the fire.

"How long do we have to stay?" Gretchen asked.

"Just let's finish this drink," I said.

I liked the sound of the crackling fire and the low voices and the occasional whoops. It was like being on a merry-go-round, knowing that the circular platform you were on divided you from a more mundane world. I liked the girls' soft nudging giggles and the robust edge to the boys' voices. One boy recounted a story about a pickerel he'd caught in the annual Gilead Fishing Derby that week. In another corner, a girl hooted over a Little Moron joke. The air seemed full of currents, whirling in all directions, but they weren't immediately detectable. You had to watch and listen hard to see where they were going.

"I'm going to go down to the water," said Gretchen. "Coming?"

I shook my head.

I found a wire wiener stick made out of a coat hanger, stuck a marshmallow on the end, and edged closer to a group standing around Rosemary. The fire was still too large for proper roasting, but I tried anyway, keeping the marshmallow just at the edge of the coals.

Voices drifted past me, through me.

"My parents say it's against the church," one girl said. "They say the Pope's against the strike."

"How do you get that?" someone asked. "What bloody business is it of the Pope's?"

"They say on socialized medicine the doctors will be paid by the state to disobey all the papal dictates. You know, about birth control and stuff."

"That's the most ridiculous thing I've ever heard," said another voice. It belonged to Lillian Keripat, the pharmacist's daughter. She'd graduated from Grade Twelve that June and planned to go to university in Saskatoon in September to study pharmacy.

"My folks call it 'a shameless political power play,'" said Kenneth Ponych, who would be one of the instructors in the Red Cross swimming lessons that were to start the following week.

"I've got a cousin in Estevan," said a boy I didn't know. "He says they're basically running the doctors out of town there. Issuing death threats to them and everything."

"Ah," said Kenneth. "The Citizens' Safety Committee. I've heard about them."

"What does running the doctors out of town have to do with citizens' safety?" asked one girl.

"They didn't run them out of town, stupid. The letters just said that if they didn't go back to work their families could be harmed."

"Well, that sounds like the same thing to me," said the girl.

My marshmallow was perfectly roasted on one side. I kept it carefully above the coals.

"I'm glad nothing like that is happening here," said Lillian.

"I feel sorry for the doctors."

"Why is that?" Arlene asked. She was sitting cross-legged on one of the ties, somewhat apart from the group.

"Think about it," Lillian said. "They have to take the Hippocratic oath, right? Then this strike comes up, and their own association clamps right down. Tells them they're breaking an act of faith if they treat their own patients. If you ask me, the doctors are between a rock and a hard place."

"That rock being Arizona," said Arlene. "The hard place likely being Hawaii."

Everyone laughed. This was before the advent of cheap air charters. Even I managed to feel a stab of envy when Gretchen returned from Christmas breaks with suntans that made my winter-wan skin even more pathetic in comparison.

"There she goes!"

They were all looking at me. I'd let the marshmallow drop too close to the coals. It was in flames.

I dashed away from the circle and tried to extinguish the fire by waving the marshmallow furiously back and forth. This only made it burn all the more, a bright orange ribbon against the fading light.

When the marshmallow stopped burning, I held it close to my face and lifted off the charred edge. Beneath the black coating, the inner core was soft and sweet. I popped the blackened top into my mouth, then lifted the sticky gooey centre onto my fingers and licked them clean.

To my surprise everyone around the fire started clapping.

The truth came to me in a rush, as it often does, the way a

smouldering driftwood twig will suddenly burst into flames. They'd clapped because they'd seen I wasn't perfect. I'd broken into the circle, if only for a moment, not because I was clean and neat and cheerful, but because I had been inattentive and careless. Because I was flawed, as they knew they were, and because I had the sense to laugh with them about those flaws. Because, for once, I'd been cool.

I ran my tongue over the inside of my mouth and my teeth, and sucked away the last sugary sweetness.

I looked around for Gretchen, expecting to see her somewhere along the shore, but she wasn't there. At least I don't remember her being there.

I turned back to the circle. I didn't know then how to be generous, or how to set myself at ease, let alone anyone else.

Saturday Morning,
JULY 7, 1962

"And how was the party?" my mother asked. She placed a box of Cocoa Puffs on the breakfast table.

"Okay."

A thousand miles southwest, at Camp Mercury, Nevada, the atmosphere still radiated from the detonation of the first hydrogen bomb in North America. Later, I'd think about that, about the cancers slowly developing, and how no one knew. And I'd realize that most of the time we can't measure danger because it's invisible. We might notice it at first, but then it thins and becomes transparent and starts to surround us in our daily lives, until we don't notice that it's there. And all the time it's growing, like my bitterness toward Gretchen that summer.

"I didn't hear you come in." Curiosity twitched in her voice.

"It was late. After twelve."

"Ah."

My parents never attempted to impose curfews on me. If

anything, they encouraged me to set my own schedules. I once overheard my mother explaining to Aunt Stina that "the more you treat a child as a responsible adult, the more the child will behave as a responsible adult."

This freedom encouraged me to view life as a continual round of decision making, an agony I discovered I could often escape by following those around me. At times the net of restrictions that bound my classmates appeared enviable. Gretchen had to be in bed by ten o'clock on school nights, and was required to make her allowance last the week. This was not the case with me, nor could I have been called a spoiled child. It was simply that I was treated as one would treat a small, dependent, rational adult. And yet I knew I was far from being an adult, rational or irrational.

Already the day had a ragged feeling. My father was reading Friday's paper. "Gov't Hints Special Session May Be Held," said the headline on the front page. A special session of the legislature was being considered if the doctors didn't go back to their practices within a few days, he said. "Living Costs at Record Level," proclaimed another headline.

The Cocoa Puffs bobbed in a sea of milk. Outside the wind whined around the corner. The sky boiled with grey clouds; the waves driven across the lake were scalloped with brittle-looking whitecaps. No one was out on the water or on the beach.

I thought of our house back in Gilead, with its wall-to-wall beige carpet in the living room and the Electrohome television set and the high caragana hedge that protected the backyard from the prevailing westerlies, and the telephone and the public library that was open all Saturday afternoon. I'd almost finished *Rilla of Ingleside Farm*.

"I hope it calms down by tonight," my mother said. She'd planned a surprise anniversary party for Uncle Gisli and Aunt Stina at their cabin.

"I think I'll go into town today," my father said. "Get a few chores done. Anyone want to come?"

"I do," said my mother. "I may as well do some work in the garden. Yours could actually use a little work too, Thora."

I'd planted a little garden plot of my own behind the garage, cornflowers mostly, and a few radishes and sweet peas in wavering rows.

"I promised I'd help Gretchen with her grasshoppers," I said.

"That's fine. We could wait if you won't be too long."

For a moment I thought I saw myself in her approving eyes. I felt her faith in my compliance as a hard, bitter stone in my mouth.

"No, I can't," I said.

My mother looked up, eyes bright.

"It's going to take all day," I said, although I knew it wouldn't.

"No matter," said my mother. "Of course, do what you promised."

She slapped bread crumbs off the plastic tablecloth and caught them with a swift movement of her hands. I could see that it mattered little to her whether I went to town with her or not. What mattered was that I preserve the picture she carried of my perfection, a picture that was fuzzy around the edges, like an ill-focused photograph, one I hoped she would not examine too closely.

I knocked on the door of the McConnells' cabin at eleven o'clock that Saturday. Both the Buick and Alexia's fire-engine red Volkswagen Beetle were gone.

The wind still swept in fiercely from the west, scissoring through my kangaroo sweat top and leaving an icy chill. The screen door had to be pulled tight so it wouldn't slam back and forth. A few years before, snow had fallen in Gilead in mid-July, a brisk flurry that was over in fifteen minutes and melted within an hour. That unseasonable winter footprint planted itself over my consciousness for the rest of my adolescent summers, so that each warm day retained a hint of fragility for me, like rose crystal.

Finally Gretchen opened the door. She wore a long flannel nightie printed with pink-cheeked cherubs floating on puffy clouds. Spots of orange juice stained the bodice. Her tangled hair fell on her shoulders in uncombed chunks.

"What do you want?" she asked, her voice so soft I had to strain to hear. She fixed her gaze somewhere beyond my right shoulder.

"I've come to help you with the grasshoppers."

"It's all right. I can do them myself."

I clutched the screen door. The cold air was entering the

cabin, blowing at the folds in Gretchen's nightie. Her feet were bare. The idea of entering that warm cabin and spending the afternoon with Gretchen suddenly seemed the most desirable and the most unattainable thing in the world.

"I thought you said you needed me," I said. I looked at my feet.

"I didn't appreciate what you did last night." Voice still soft and gauzy as eiderdown.

"I didn't do anything."

"You promised we wouldn't stay long."

"I just wanted to stay by the fire for a few minutes more."

"Well, anyway," said Gretchen. "I can do the hoppers myself. It'll just take me a little more time."

She closed the door gently.

I turned back to the road. There still weren't any signs of activity; almost everyone must have gone into Gilead for the day.

I didn't want to stay at the lake, and I didn't want to go into town. I felt as if a vacuum had opened up inside me and was sucking the oxygen out of my blood vessels. One way to escape, I thought, would be to become caught in a whirlwind, the kind that lifted dust from farmers' fields on days like this and twisted it into harmless funnels high into the sky. I remembered how, when I was younger, I used to run across a field of summerfallow towards such whirlwinds, hoping to be caught in the eye of one and to fly above the clouds.

What I wanted now was nothing less than to escape gravity, to swirl above the rickety little cabins and the rheumy, gaping eye of Whitefish Lake, and be cleansed by air that had been kissed by the Polar Cap.

To hell with Gretchen.

The wind seemed to hurtle me down the road, past our cabin, past Aunt Stina's. A couple of cars were parked in front of the confectionery at the golf course where the beach road curved to join the secondary highway into town. Along with chocolate bars and pop, the store sold a few over-large golf shirts and baseball caps and bathing suits. It occurred to me to have a look at them.

I scarcely heard the car draw up behind me.

"Hey, Sigurdson, want a lift?"

It was Rosemary, driving her mother's red-and-black Chev. Arlene was in the passenger's seat. The twins were wearing dangly earrings of pink plastic that matched their lipstick. On Rosemary the combination seemed jaunty, but I thought it made Arlene look lifeless, the pink prettiness of the jewellery at odds with the determined set of her jaw and her habitually blank expression.

The wind beat into my face, and darker patches of cloud scudded across the western horizon. Rosemary had the radio turned low, Bobby Vinton crooning "Roses are Red," his voice sweet and inviting, just as the voices by the fire had been the night before.

"I'm just out for a walk," I started to say. The truth was that I relished fresh air. I rejoiced in the wind and the cold and other inclement weather most people complained about and that my mother approvingly called "bracing."

But even as I uttered those words, I could picture the Chev driving away. I could envision the exact shape of its tail lights, winking at me like seductive red eyes as they signalled a right turn in the distance, and I could see myself, as well, abandoned on the gusty dirt road. My parents wouldn't be back for hours. The time until their return gaped before me like unknown territory on a map.

There was another thing too, an edge in Rosemary's voice barely discernible beneath her thick, smooth, overfriendly manner. I understood that if I didn't accept the twins' invitation to join them, I would not be asked again.

I climbed into the back seat of the Chevy. It was all vinyl, without any pile covering or even a horsehair rug to make the seat more comfortable. But the floor mats were clean, the windows spotless, and the chrome around the windows gleamed.

"So did you enjoy the party last night?" Rosemary asked. She drove with one hand and kept time to the music with the other, the way Alexia did.

"Yeah, it was fun," I said.

"The doctor's brat didn't stay long." Arlene's voice. She didn't bother to turn back to look at me when she spoke. "Didn't she enjoy our company?"

"She wasn't feeling very well."

I hadn't planned to lie. The words just came out of me. Until the day before, Gretchen had been the one to protect me, usually from my own stupidities. She'd help me finish biology homework at the last minute when I couldn't figure out the answer, or lend me her extra pair of white gym shorts when I forgot mine. She didn't always come to my rescue graciously. Sometimes she reminded me of my folly for weeks afterward. But she had never refused to help me when I asked.

My words seemed to hang in the air for a long time. It wasn't until much later that I understood why. It was because those words didn't make me feel brave or loyal. They made me feel small and mean, as if I could reduce our friendship to a mouthful of sounds and toss them out wherever I wanted to.

"So she was sick," said Rosemary, nodding. I couldn't tell if she believed me. This time Arlene turned around and gave me a withering look.

The wind seemed to be gathering force, bending the young aspens almost at right angles, so that they looked like greenclad medieval courtiers bowing.

Rosemary turned onto the secondary road. They were just out for a joyride, she said. We would go where the roads took us.

"Are you going to the pavilion tonight?" she asked.

I shook my head.

Dances were held every Saturday night in summer at the pavilion on the other side of the lake. Sometimes big bands came from Regina and Saskatoon and Winnipeg. I didn't want to go. The place had a reputation for drinking and fights between gangs from surrounding towns. Besides, I had no idea how to dance.

"We could give you a lift," said Rosemary. I thought I saw her wink at Arlene.

"No thanks," I said. "I have to go to my aunt's anniversary."

"Oh well," said Arlene. She turned right around in her seat, so she was facing me. "You're good friends with the McConnells, right?" she asked.

"I guess so."

"We were just wondering. Some of us, that is. Is the doc still treating any patients on the side? Have you any idea?"

I thought of the man's voice I'd heard the other evening.

"I wouldn't know," I said. "He's been going to a lot of meetings, I think, since the strike started."

"I guess. Do me a favour?"

"Yeah?"

"If you find out that he's treating any patients, could you let Rosemary and me know? Doctors aren't supposed to do that now, except in emergencies. That group – what do you call it – College of Physicians and Surgeons, I think, says they're not supposed to. That's what Mom says anyway."

Rosemary swung out onto another secondary road. We were speeding by the mixed farms, in the direction of Gilead.

I thought of Mac, with his easy manner and quick encouragements.

"You mean, be a spy?" I said.

"I mean, be a good citizen."

"I don't follow."

"Look," Arlene said. "Do I have to spell it out? This is an illegal strike against the Saskatchewan public."

I would like to say that I asked Rosemary to let me out

then, but I didn't. I shrugged, and I allowed silence to be my answer, because she and Arlene could interpret my silence any way they wanted.

We drove nearly to Gilead, then turned back. The twins left me off at the confectionery, but by then I didn't want to look at bathing suits.

Some joyride.

Saturday Evening,
JULY 7, 1962

Aunt Stina wore a necklace of white pearls that evening, a wedding present from Uncle Gisli, and even though she had gained thirty pounds, the pearls gave her face a delicate, wistful look. The wind had dropped. Earlier I'd helped my parents carry cold ham-and-egg sandwiches and an extra coffee percolator over to Aunt Stina's for the anniversary party.

About two dozen people chatted on the deck while Uncle Gisli and my father started putting up card tables for whist. The mayor of Gilead was there, the reeve of the rural municipality, several members of the Elks Lodge, which Uncle Gisli had belonged to for twenty years, and women from Aunt Stina's bridge club and the hospital auxiliary. I was the only teenager, but I was accustomed to this. My parents often took me along to visit with friends and relatives, and almost always the children of the people they visited would have grown up years before. I doubt if it ever occurred to my parents that I might be bored on these visits, and in fact I learned to enjoy the adults' gossip, and the way they seemed to forget my presence when they talked.

The last tables had been set up when the phone rang. The Johnsons were among the few people at the lake who had a telephone. My aunt went to answer it. When she returned, her neck was flushed.

"Isn't that awful?" she said. "That was Alexia, ringing to say she and Mac won't be coming after all. Dr. Sullivan died of a heart attack tonight. Just collapsed right in the hospital. You know Dr. Sullivan? The doctor at Teasdale?"

Most people knew that Dr. Sullivan was one of Dr. McConnell's best friends. They'd emigrated together to Saskatchewan from Scotland.

"Only fifty years old," Aunt Stina said. "They think it was because of the stress from the strike." She paused. "Teasdale being the only emergency clinic open between here and Saskatoon, you know."

There were low murmurings of consolation. Several of the guests had been treated by Dr. Sullivan, whom I recalled as a friendly man with vivid red hair.

I didn't want to play whist, so before long I walked back to my parents' cabin. Music from the pavilion drifted across the lake. I couldn't make out the lyrics, or even the song. It was the first time I'd heard music from the pavilion, and it occurred to me that it must have been there all along, in the airwaves on Saturday nights, but I simply hadn't been attuned to it before.

I thought of the kids over at the pavilion, likely some of the ones who had been at the beach party the night before, only a little older than I was, and of Rosemary and the easy way she laughed and how she would have gone to the dance with no fear, armed with the certain knowledge that she would enjoy herself. I wondered about Arlene too – if she enjoyed the dances at the pavilion, or if she accompanied Rosemary because that was the only way she would ever be part of such a fun-loving crowd.

And I wondered about Gretchen. I hadn't seen her since that morning. I wondered if she was in the porch, sorting hoppers, or reading in her high bunk with its view over the lake. And I remembered something she'd told me once, that in a perfect world she would always be a child, because then things would always be new to her, and that Thomas Hardy, whom she admired, had shared that wish and so there must be nothing wrong with it. I wondered if she ever heard the music from the pavilion.

Sunday Morning,
JULY 8, 1962

Out in the middle of the lake, Old Unfaithful rocked like a tap dancer's shoe, black and sleek. I picked up the binoculars for a closer look. That's what I always seemed to be doing. Watching. Listening.

It was the day after the anniversary party. Usually summer Sundays at the lake had a festive feel, as if we were all determined to cram a year's leisure into our few guaranteed frost-free weekends. But that day, bruise-coloured clouds hid the sun and a northwest breeze bent the gangly weeds pushing up on the beach. I'd woken to the sound of the wind teasing the window at the end of my bunk and my parents driving off to church in Gilead. "The least we can do," my mother had said the night before. "So many people are away, the church will be three-quarters empty."

I was alone in the cabin. The floor was cold. The only sound was the wind. The corners of the one large room that served as the combined kitchen, dining room, and living room struck me as dark and best avoided. Cool drafts knifed in when the wind gusted. Altogether it was a delicious feeling, sitting at the dining table turning the pages of the magazines Aunt Stina had lent my mother the night before: *Chatelaine, Redbook,* the *Star Weekly, Look.* I sensed that I was marooned, but safe. Out of sight, but watchful.

There wasn't much to see. No one had appeared on the beach or the lake except Alexia, carrying her fishing rod in one arm and a tackle box in the other. Half an hour earlier, I'd watched her push Old Unfaithful away from the dock. She gave the black speedboat that name because, she said, the eighty-five horsepower motor was "not consistently faithful."

She'd covered her hair with a white kerchief, knotted at the nape, and wore blue jeans and a navy nylon windbreaker. After she gunned the engine, the prow bounced up and down against the green waves, sending great spumes of water flying. I remembered how Alexia refused to slow down for bumps on the road. She enjoyed taking Old Unfaithful out on her own, unlike some of the women on the beach who only got into boats as passengers. She said she'd learned to do a lot of things alone, being a doctor's wife. And yet she had a way of seeming helpless. When she couldn't figure out how to detach the grass catcher from the lawn mower the other night, she'd asked my father to come over. I ran ahead and detached it myself before he got there.

Next door, Vivienne Krywulak carried an armful of tea towels to hang on the line between our cabins. Rosemary was behind her. She limped slightly. She hung up two or three towels and left her mother to do the rest.

Vivienne wore a thin green cotton print dress; her arms were bare. She hugged them as she ran back to the cabin. I never saw her in the water, and only on the beach on the warmest days, when she suntanned and read thick paperbacks like *The Carpetbaggers*. Often at such times, my mother would call out when she'd made afternoon coffee and Vivienne would come into the cabin, bringing with her the scent of toasting flesh. They would chat for half an hour or so over my mother's date bars and macaroons. Vivienne hadn't been over, however, since the strike began.

More than once I'd seen Jerry Embury's Ford pickup at Vivienne's early in the morning, before anyone else was up. Jerry was a tall, thin man of about forty who didn't seem to have much to say to children, even though he'd just got a job driving the school bus between Gilead and Whitefish Lake for swimming lessons. Sometimes he walked stiffly, and was said to have damaged a spinal disc at his last job. Uncle Gisli said he'd had to fire Jerry from his job at the lumberyard because he'd come into work once too often "stewed to the gills," and that any accident he had was probably his own bloody fault. I usually believed what my uncle said. My mother said Uncle Gisli knew the currents of town like a well-witcher.

When Old Unfaithful vanished from sight, I opened the book Alexia had dropped off for me the day before: *Master-crafting Miniature Pioneer Structures*. An hour passed, maybe more, before I raised my head.

When I next looked out, a few drops of rain splattered the front windowpane. Old Unfaithful was bobbing far out from shore, a blurry black dot against tin sky that dissolved into tin water. I could see a figure in the stern – Alexia – bending over the outboard. Whitecaps rolled under Old Unfaithful's hull. Still no one appeared on the beach or on the water. Alexia remained hunched over the engine for several minutes. I sensed stubbornness in her spine.

She moved forward into the driver's seat, removed the white scarf from her head and began waving it.

I knew it wouldn't take long for someone with a boat to notice and come to the rescue. Not that Gretchen was likely to see her mother out there; no doubt she was in her room, identifying flora and fauna or studying ancient dam engineering. I hadn't seen Gretchen since Saturday morning, and the coolness of her brown eyes when she shut the screen door against me still gnawed at my nerves. I couldn't help thinking that she had worn the same expression when she sealed a killing jar.

Someone would come to Alexia's rescue. The waves weren't that big anyway. I knew with certainty she would be rescued, as I knew with certainty that it wasn't up to me to do so. I couldn't pull the cord hard enough to start our engine.

I opened *Mastercrafting Miniatures* and turned the radio on at low volume. CBC 540 in Regina was broadcasting a special roundup on the Saskatchewan strike. I only half listened. Usually at eleven o'clock on Sunday mornings the radio programming was filled with reports from other, more exciting parts of the world, places like Detroit where auto workers were threatening to strike if an auto-pact agreement wasn't signed, or the Soviet Union, where cosmonauts were preparing to orbit into outer space, or Boston, where the strangler had struck again.

But that morning was different. Dr. William Cusp, the head of legal medicine at Tufts University in Boston, came on the air. His name has stayed with me all these years. A fitting name. We were all on the cusp that summer, and didn't know it. Dr. Cusp, the interviewer said in his introduction, had offered his services to investigate any deaths in Saskatchewan that might be related to what the report called "professional negligence by delinquent physicians."

Years later, I looked up the doctor's exact words. They had been reported at length in the Regina *Leader-Post* and were easy to find on microfiche. The American doctor said that although he was available to investigate cases of possible professional negligence in Saskatchewan, he "held no brief for socialized medicine. It quells initiative, imprisons freedom of thought, and negates the essentials of research."

I stopped reading the book on miniatures and sat there with an old puzzle replaying in my head. Saskatchewan took up so much space on the atlas, more than a dozen American states or most of the United Kingdom. Yet it was almost never mentioned in the magazines Aunt Stina lent us, or on television or radio reports outside the province, except for the occasional mention of foreign grain sales or minus-forty-degree weather or jokes about Moose Jaw.

I wish I could say that I thought again about Alexia, out on the lake, and at least went to the window to make certain someone was helping her. But I didn't. I was just so entranced by my miniatures book, and by the astonishing things I was hearing on the radio. It seemed that people from all over – important people – were paying attention to what was happening in our province. Here was Dr. Cusp, saying that Saskatchewan had become a laboratory test for the future of the free world. If the citizens of the province let their government get away with its plan to shackle doctors into a universal medicare plan, he said, the sanctity of the physician-patient relationship throughout North America, and perhaps the free world, would be threatened.

The sanctity of the free world? Could I have heard him right?

I thought about the grasshoppers in Gretchen's killing jar, and how she said she needed to sacrifice them in the quest for knowledge, and I wondered if Dr. Cusp could possibly mean that the people of Saskatchewan were like those hoppers, haplessly jumping around while above our heads, unknown to us, someone was putting the lid on our freedom.

Surely he couldn't mean that.

Another voice came on the air. It belonged to a columnist for the *Washington Daily Post* who said that Saskatchewan was "sick, sick, sick." He pronounced it Sask-AT-CHOO-an. The strike, he said, had shocked all of the United States and Canada. "It would require the service of a whole squad of social psychiatrists to determine how nine hundred physicians could have turned to sadists. They have decided to punish the eight hundred thousand people of Saskatchewan for voting to set up what they, the people, consider a desirable form of medical economics."

After that I stopped listening. It was too confusing. I knew what a sadist was. The Boston Strangler, who had just struck again, was a sadist. Not Dr. McConnell. It was equally hard for me to believe what Dr. Cusp had said, about the future of the free world being determined here, in our quiet province with its grain elevators and little towns and only two big cities, Saskatoon and Regina, which Uncle Gisli said were so small they might be called towns in the United States. A few years before, I'd been the envy of Gilead because I possessed the first Hula Hoop; Aunt Stina had brought it back for me from one of her trips to California. When my father had wanted to buy an automatic stone-picker a few years before, he hadn't been able to get one in Canada and had to drive across the border to Minot, North Dakota, to find one. I knew what these things meant, although I'd never been to the United States myself. In that country everything was bigger, brighter, louder, less expensive, and better than what we had in Canada.

I still didn't think about checking on Alexia, or about seeing if I could get someone else to help her. I was just so sure that someone would. Instead I turned back to my reading. The book on miniatures said that almost all houses are made of the same building materials: timbers, shingles, bricks, stones, windows, doors, and mouldings. What makes them unique is the way the basic materials are put together. I hadn't thought of houses that way before; I'd viewed them as being grand or plain, or in-between, as most of the houses in Gilead were. If what the book said was true, any plain house could be a palace. All that was required was that it be constructed with sufficient care and imagination and artistry.

I found this cheering.

I was still reading when my parents returned from church. The truth is, I'd forgotten all about Alexia. It seemed as if only a few minutes had passed, although by twelve-thirty I'd read five chapters.

Old Unfaithful was a speck on the water. Alexia still waved her scarf, although her waving arm wasn't held high any more. The wind whipped the water as fiercely as ever. Whitecaps extended right across to Walema Beach.

"What the deuce?" my father asked. "How long has she been out there?"

He left the cabin door open behind him and went straight for the binoculars.

"I don't know," I said.

"Looks like she's having the devil of a time." My father scowled at me. "What the Sam Hill have you been doing, Thora? Sitting there like Miss Bo Peep. Didn't you see her out there?"

"Yes, but...."

"Then why the Christ didn't you get someone to help?"

Never before had my father sworn at me. Even invoking Sam Hill, whoever he might be, could be cause for alarm. "I'm sorry," I said. "I thought for sure somebody would help."

My father wasn't listening. He was already in the bunk room, grabbing a life jacket. I watched as he hurried down to the dock. Vivienne Krywulak's tea towels swung wildly in the breeze.

Sunday Afternoon,
JULY 8, 1962

Alexia knocked on the door of the cabin shortly after lunch. I was drying the dishes while my parents rested. It was my only regular household chore.

A light rain beat upon the windows. On dull days like this, the light inside the cabin took on a ghastly hue, a blend of cheap home-mixed Latex and the bare light bulb that shone in the middle of the ceiling.

"I won't come in," Alexia said in a soft voice. "I just wondered – it looks as though that rainy day has come. Want to start on the miniature this afternoon?"

"Oh, yes."

She must have caught a look of surprise on my face. My cheeks felt warm. At that moment I wished more than anything that I was the kind of girl my parents thought I was, instead of the silly, distracted, daydreaming girl I knew myself to be.

"You're thinking I don't exactly look like the damsel in distress," she laughed. "Well, I certainly felt like one for a while this morning."

"I'm sorry I didn't help," I said. "I thought you'd be okay."

"I was, I was," Alexia said. "You'll come over, then?"

"I'd love to."

It hadn't taken my father long to tow Old Unfaithful back to shore; now he was sleeping on the sofa. A recent bulletin on recommended summerfallow practices from the University of Saskatchewan's agriculture extension department was slumped on his chest. It rose and fell gently with his breathing.

After their naps, my parents planned to go back to the Johnsons' for an afternoon of canasta. I scribbled a note saying where I'd gone and left it on the table.

I didn't know how to make miniatures, but once Aunt Stina had given me a set of Lego building blocks that linked together and could be used to make houses with different styles of roofs, or even a gas station. Of course I had become too old to play with the Lego, but I kept all the pieces on a shelf in the basement in Gilead.

I found Gretchen in the living room at the McConnells', not locked away in her room as I'd expected.

"Glad you could come over," Alexia said. "It's a dull, rotten day, isn't it? Did you hear about Dr. Sullivan?"

I nodded. Her smile was so warm I felt touched by light.

"Dad had to go to Teasdale. We're all on our own."

"We won't be able to enlist her in miniatures, though," Alexia said. "She's only agreed to supervise."

Gretchen, in fact, planned nothing of the kind. She had brought down an encyclopedia of South American moths and set it up on a card table in front of the big armchair where she sat. She'd talked for a long time about how she wanted to spend an afternoon with that book, because she thought she could understand so much more about native insects if she knew more about related species which had been studied longer.

"Maybe after we could go for a walk," she said. "When it stops raining."

She placed her chin on her hand, in a gesture I'd become accustomed to, and propped the book up on her knees. I knew her well enough by then to realize how quickly she could be transported to a place where I couldn't follow. Her joyrides were different from those of Rosemary and her friends, because most of her travelling was done inside her head, and it would have been hard for me to say which type of abandonment made me feel more bereft.

Gretchen could be companionable one minute, distant the next, angry, then happy, as changeable in her way as her hoppers: all jump and then quiet as a corpse. But even when she seemed quiet I could sense her power to spring. Compared to her, I felt as dull and predictable as a cabbage moth, flitting back and forth in the slightest breeze, in no way remarkable.

Alexia led me into the back porch. "See, I've just made a small beginning," she said.

She kept a long table there, made of a battered old door set on two sawhorses, where she often worked on her enthusiasms of the moment: papier mâché, eggshell decoration, tiny portrait frames laboriously constructed from glued snail shells.

On that day, she'd set out a rectangular square of freshly sawn plywood, a sheet of scaled paper, a ruler tape measure and two sharp pencils. "I thought we'd use this as the foundation," she said. "We can probably fashion the actual logs from those." She pointed to a pile of twigs on one corner of the table.

We stood beside the table, looking down at the scaled paper. "Let's each have a go, and see what we come up with," she said.

I wasn't good at math or measurements, but I liked looking at that paper and thinking of it as a pathway that would lead to a finished miniature. I knew that without Alexia I would simply have stumbled ahead, sawing away at branches and twigs, mixing plaster, hoping that somehow it would all fall into a vision I had in my head. And it wouldn't have, of course, because the vision in my head was incomplete.

"Take your time," Alexia said. "Build it any way you want."

The rain stopped about five o'clock, in time for Gretchen and me to have a short walk together down the road. She lent me an emerald Ban-Lon sweater, since the air was still cold. Milky light shone all along the edges of the horizon, then deepened into blues and greys. The air smelled as clean as peppermint.

As we were leaving, a blue Ford pickup truck drove up in front of the McConnells'. Jerry Embury got out.

"Your dad in?" he asked Gretchen.

"No," she said.

The flag was down. Anyone who paid any attention would have known that Mac wasn't at the cabin.

"When'll he be back?"

"I'm not sure," she said.

I recognized his voice. It was the one I'd heard speaking to Mac a few nights before. Jerry was the man Mac had asked to keep quiet about the treatments he'd received from the doctor during the strike.

"Well," he said, "I'll check back later."

Gretchen didn't say anything. She often forgot to say hello or goodbye to people, because her mind jumped ahead so quickly.

When Jerry got back in the truck, she turned to me. "Pathetic, isn't he? He's the reason Dad had to fire Vivienne Krywulak. Stupid cow."

Gretchen rarely spoke of her father's patients or employees. She was naturally discreet and, besides that, she had little interest in town gossip.

I didn't say anything, hoping she'd go on. I liked gossip. I liked thinking about what people did when they thought other people wouldn't know.

This time, Gretchen didn't disappoint me. Mac had caught

Vivienne trying to fake his signature on some Workmen's Compensation Board forms for Jerry, she said. "Of course Daddy had to fire her right on the spot, once he knew he couldn't trust her. There's nothing serious enough about Jerry's injuries to keep him off work, although he did pull a couple of muscles."

I wanted her to say more, but by that time Gretchen's mind had jumped ahead once again.

"Let's go to swimming lessons together tomorrow," she said. As usual, she managed to surprise me. I wasn't even sure she'd planned to take Red Cross swimming lessons. She'd had to take Intermediate lessons for two years, and even then barely managed to get her badge the year before.

"Sure," I said. Stepping back into our friendship was as welcome to me as a warm wave of lake water on a sunny day. It buoyed me and shook me at the same time.

I still believe that, although I can't be sure. Memories are like that; they filter through the mental, scribbled-over tablets of the past like strobes of light under water, pausing here or there, unable to cast into focus the hieroglyphics they find and leaving only shadows and fuzzy edges. The heart's eraser.

Just before supper, the six o'clock news reported that a prominent economics professor from the University of Saskatchewan thought a special session of the legislature should be held immediately to repeal the medical care act.

The act, the professor claimed in a deep, calm voice, had created "chaotic conditions" throughout the province and would cause more unnecessary deaths if not repealed soon.

My parents spoke little during the meal. Their afternoon had been uneventful, they said. If it weren't for swimming lessons starting the next day, they'd be tempted to pack up and go back to town for a few days.

For a long time after the dishes had been cleared away, my father stayed at the kitchen table. He looked out at the lake, which had a translucent sheen on it, as if illuminated from the depths. Once in a while, he furiously wrote numbers on a scrap of paper.

"Twelve-odd," he said finally. "I'd betcha twelve-odd."

"Twelve-odd what?" My mother looked up from the afghan she was crocheting for the Ladies Hospital Auxiliary handicraft sale in September.

"Twelve-odd people who must have seen Alexia stranded out there this morning. And who didn't lift a finger."

Then he scowled at me. "Thirteen if we count you, Thora. Which we should. I'm ashamed of you."

"I'm sure she feels bad enough, Bjorn," my mother said. "Don't you, Thora?"

"Yes," I said. "I feel terrible."

"So you should," my father said. "You could have asked Bert Paulson. He was out back, working in his garage this morning."

My father looked at me again, his brows knitted. "It would have taken you two minutes to have run over and told him

Alexia was in trouble."

I couldn't look my father in the face. He had figured it all
out: how many cabins fronted West Beach, how many
summer residents were away or likely to have been in church
that morning. That left twelve men with motorboats who had
likely seen Alexia out on the water and ignored her.

He tapped his fingers on the arborite table. Finally he
turned to my mother.

"We'd better go to Regina next week with Stina and Gisli,"
he said. "It's our duty to stand up for what we think. We
damned well don't want socialized medicine in this province."

My mother stopped crocheting for a moment. "Besides,"
she said, "Mac is our friend."

I wanted to feel proud that my parents had decided to go to
the rally, that they were the kind of people who would
protest against what the government was trying to do to doctors because they thought it was wrong, and because they
believed in standing up for their friends.

But I felt uneasy, not proud. I went up to my bunk and
looked at an article in *Seventeen* magazine on fall make-overs
for students, and wondered if I could ever get a haircut that
swung as evenly as those of the models in the pictures. One of
the models reminded me of Rosemary, except that all her
teeth were perfectly straight.

Monday Morning,
JULY 9, 1962

The yellow noses of the school buses from Gilead, bright as sunflowers, eased into place in the parking lot above the public beach.

Gretchen and I were walking along the shore of Whitefish Lake to the Red Cross swimming lessons. "Aren't you glad we don't have to spend our summers in town?" I asked.

"Yes," Gretchen said in her precise way. "I shouldn't very much care to be there over summer vac. It's jolly living out here in the warm weather. Rather like a safari, really. A Saskatchewan safari."

Neither Gretchen nor I had experienced a summer in town, but we could imagine from the throngs of children that clamoured for a ride to the lake on the school buses during the ten days of swimming lessons. Gilead had few recreational facilities, aside from the skating and curling rink. The tennis courts hadn't been used since my mother was in her twenties. By July, waist-high Russian thistle overran the corner lots where children played softball and cricket on the long spring nights. The wading pool had cracked years before and not been repaired. Most girls our age, we suspected, spent July and August babysitting or thumbing through the new Eaton's or Simpson-Sears winter catalogues. Yet we knew that Gilead was no less eventful than the other towns of its size, strung out like beads on a necklace along the Canadian Pacific Railway line between Winnipeg and Saskatoon. In fact, Gilead, with its jaunty annual Agricultural Fair in August and the sequin-studded Winter Carnival in February, likely offered a wider range of activity than many neighbouring towns. Pleasure, though, seemed on the whole to be reserved for special days, special times.

Mac remarked on this soon after he arrived in Gilead, which is why building the Rec Centre took most of his energy during his first two years in town. When that was finished, he formed a steering committee to raise money for a municipal swimming pool. The new pool was going to be built in Gilead Community Park, right in the centre of town. The committee had already reached one-third of its goal through car washes and raffles and bingos, but it would be at least a year before construction began.

In the meantime, Red Cross swimming lessons offered the town kids one of their few diversions during the summer. The classes were always jammed; almost every kid in town signed up, whether or not they had any interest in swimming. Our schoolmate Susan Mellers, who rode the bus each day, said the town kids began to gather in the public schoolyard before eight every morning during lessons, although the bus didn't leave until eight-thirty.

Gretchen and I didn't talk much on our walk that morning, but our silence held a sense of healing. I realized that she had not only forgiven me for ignoring her at the Krywulaks' beach party, but had most likely forgotten about the entire episode. And yet she could remember so many things. Like the average maturation times for all the species of hoppers in Western Canada. And whether or not flatworms were hermaphroditic. I, on the other hand, had no head for scientific facts and figures. But I could remember every petty slight ever given me.

By the time we reached the public beach, the beginners were already in the water. Feathered clouds flocked the whole sky, the sun promised warmth, and a light breeze shoved brisk little waves from shore. A few younger teenagers, thirteen- and fourteen-year-olds like ourselves, had grouped themselves in twosomes and threesomes along the beach, reading paper-backs and talking and applying suntan lotion. Up by the buses, the drivers stood in the shade of scattered poplars. They wore long flannel pants, short-sleeved plaid shirts, and leather shoes. I recognized one of them as Jerry Embury. He and the other man smoked and kicked at the tires.

Gretchen and I found a spot high on the beach to spread our blanket. Gretchen's skin burned easily too, even though she applied Coppertone copiously, and unlike me she wanted to stay out of the sun. If one mosquito was in a room, she would be the one bitten. "I like the outdoors," she'd laugh, "but the outdoors doesn't like me."

A group of about ten older teenagers, those taking Senior

lessons, formed a loose circle on the left side of the beach. Rosemary's high laugh rose from the centre of the circle. "That's BS," she was telling Kenneth Ponych, one of the two Red Cross swimming instructors. "Total BS."

She held a package of Cameos in her hand, the same brand her mother smoked. I liked the way they smelled, cool and minty. When Rosemary stepped over to her beach bag for another cigarette, her limp seemed worse.

Arlene stood beside Rosemary, and then a minute later the attention of the circle shifted to her. That's what I remember, anyway. I thought this was unusual, until I realized that she was demonstrating straight arm recovery in the crawl strokes. I watched her arm swing from the shoulder, describing an arc to the point of entry for the next stroke, and it reminded me of films I'd seen of English oarsmen rowing, swinging their oars back to position to take a stroke.

Arlene had obtained her Advanced Intermediate badge in Saskatoon that spring. Everyone knew how keen she was to pass her Senior's test that summer, so she could get her instructor's certificate the following spring. Her mother had told my mother that Arlene was determined to be a lifeguard the next summer. She made no secret of the fact that she never wanted to spend her days in smelly plants the way Vivienne had to.

"I'll be back in a minute," I said.

Gretchen didn't answer. She was watching a hopper. Usually we didn't see hoppers on the beach, but that summer there were so many that the wind seemed to carry them everywhere. A few days before, when I'd been out on the lake fishing with my father, I'd even found a hopper in the tackle box.

Standing at the edge of a circle of older teenagers, I watched Arlene demonstrate the stroke once more. Of all the swimming strokes, the crawl was the one stroke I had trouble with. I didn't like the way the crawl made you surface and then go under again; I wanted to do one or the other. Arlene's motions contained a grace and fluidity I hadn't observed before, probably because most of the time Arlene paled beside Rosemary. It wasn't only that Arlene wasn't as pretty as her sister. It was more a matter of *shine.* Everything about Rosemary seemed luminous – her hair, her skin, her eyes. If she punctured her skin, I'd *expect* to see only the bright blood I saw at the accident. Arlene's blood would be the colour of rust.

I placed one arm high above my head, describing the same arc, and that's when Arlene noticed me.

"Ah," she said to the others, "little pitchers have big ears."

They all looked at me, except for Rosemary and Kenneth, who were engaged in a sand fight down by the water.

"Do we have little spies in our midst?" Arlene spoke quietly, but her eyes didn't leave mine, and her throat muscles looked tight.

A couple of people shuffled their feet in the sand. Down by the water, I could hear Rosemary giggle.

"So, tell me, Thora, is it true your dad's going to be on the doctors' side at the rally?"

I couldn't find my voice, not with all those people looking at me.

"Is it?" Arlene stepped closer, and picked up a handful of sand. "Your hair looks a little dirty. How would you like a nice shampoo?"

I knew what she had in mind, and I should have run. But I stayed where I was. I couldn't give her the pleasure of seeing my back, much as I dreaded what she had in mind. I'd heard of sand shampoos, although I'd never seen one. My father said they dated back from when he was a kid, although they'd gotten rougher since then. In a sand shampoo, a group ganged up on a victim, hurling sand until he or she could barely stand, sometimes forcing the victim's head deep into the sand before heaving him into the lake.

No one would have dared getting away with sand shampoos on our beach, but it was different on the public beach. There were no adults around, except for the instructors, who were little older than their students, and the school bus drivers, who were always so busy smoking and talking to each other that they never watched what was going on. I wanted to run. But my feet stayed where they were. I hated the idea of unfamiliar hands on my body, poking and prodding, flinging sand and grit, shouting in my ear, sand scraping my nostrils, my ears, half choking me. I started to shake.

Two words would have stopped all of it. He's not, I could say. My father's not supporting the doctors. My eyes focused on Arlene's feet. She'd painted her toenails a purplish pink.

"Cat got your tongue?" Arlene demanded.

"I don't think my parents have made up their mind, actually," I said. I tried to think of the words as a particular arrangement of wave frequencies, nothing more.

"Hey," said a voice. It was Rosemary. "She's just a kid."

Rosemary looked at Arlene. "It's still a free country, you know."

Arlene shrugged. "What the hell," she said.

I turned around and walked back to Gretchen. I made each footstep slow and deliberate. But even though I'd escaped the sand shampoo, I felt gritty.

Only seven of us showed up for Advanced Intermediate lessons: three pimply boys from town, Bill McClymont, Melvin Koschuk, and Orest Zankiw; a pale girl named Lorreen from another town, who we didn't know; Susan; Gretchen; and me. The instructor, James Harrison, a lean, serious boy with a blond brush cut, led us through a review of the strokes we'd mastered for our Intermediate badges: treading water, breaststroke, side stroke, backstroke, back float. I could do everything easily, but after five minutes of treading water, Gretchen started to cough and paddled to the instructor's platform where the water was only waist-deep.

"You'll have to work on that," said James, in a kindly tone. "Plenty of time in the next few days."

The sky clouded over and rain began spitting down halfway through our lessons. We retreated to the picnic shelter by the school buses for the last half hour before lunch, where

James demonstrated basic rope throwing and other dryland rescue methods.

By early afternoon, the sun was out again. Gretchen and I stayed on the beach chatting with Susan until she boarded the school bus at three o'clock. By this time, all the other teenagers had left. I'd seen Rosemary and Arlene get into the red convertible that Kenneth Ponych had won that winter in a Brylcreem limerick contest.

"Wanna walk back on the beach or the road?" I asked.

My question surprised me. In nice weather we almost always walked on the beach. The road was dusty and full of ruts. Sometimes boys from other towns would cruise by in rusty, dented cars and offer rides or make lewd suggestions. Maybe I was drawn to the road that afternoon because I already felt so gritty, and it didn't seem like the kind of grit that lake water could wash away.

"The beach," Gretchen said.

"You know," she said, as we approached the McConnells' cabin, "I'd really hate to move away."

"Move away?"

"Like some of the doctors in other towns are doing."

I'd heard that all four doctors in Estevan, in the south-eastern part of the province, had decided to move to Alberta. On the weekend, one newspaper carried a full-page story about a Texas doctor who had recently flown up to Saskatoon with the intention of luring Saskatchewan doctors to Houston. He said the freedom still existed in Texas to practise medicine as it should be practised. Meanwhile, more British volunteer doctors were arriving in the province every week, hired by the Saskatchewan Medical Care Commission for temporary duty during the crisis.

"You're not thinking about it, are you?" I asked. I couldn't imagine Gilead without Gretchen.

"I don't think so," she said. "I heard Dad on the phone last night saying Gilead is a sensible place. It's not like Estevan."

The Citizens' Safety Committee in Estevan had been particularly active, she said. Some of the doctors and their families had received death threats.

"You haven't had any more crank calls, have you?" I asked.

"Oh, a couple. Always a woman, the same woman. We don't take them seriously."

Both Mac and Alexia were sitting out on their patio when we got back after lessons. Mac looked tanned and robust. As usual, he was smoking a cigarette, and the ashes had burned into a long, dangerous-looking column at the tip that he either hadn't noticed or hadn't bothered to flick away.

"Ah, just the person," he said to me. He put down the *Scotsman,* which he had mailed to him in bundles every week. "Would you mind asking your mother to drop by for a moment before dinner?" He lifted his glass of lemonade, sprinkling ashes over the red-bricked patio floor. "I'm too lazy to move."

"Of course."

As I approached our cabin, I heard Rosemary's voice next door through one of the open windows. I was surprised she was back so soon. Usually she and Arlene and their friends drove to the Dairy Queen in Gilead after lessons.

"It hurts, Mom," Rosemary said.

I couldn't hear Vivienne's reply.

Her tea towels were still on the line. She'd left them there overnight.

Friday Evening,
JUNE 19, 1998

The phone is ringing when I open the door to my little Skunk Hollow bungalow.

"Everything's fine with the Olafsson House, isn't it, Thora?" Svava Erlendson asks. "I was just thinking, with the river rising so much, there might be problems."

"Everything's great," I assure her.

"Oh, well, I'm sure it is," she chirps on. "It's just that...well, you'll keep me posted, won't you?"

"Yes, of course."

"By the way, it looks as if we're getting the Snowlands Choir. They called this afternoon to confirm."

"That's wonderful." I hope my voice doesn't sound as strung out as I feel.

Svava rings off with a cheery "ta, ta, now." Yet I can't turf the leakage problem out of my mind. As I eat my Italian takeout (right from the box, my standards are hitting bottom since Paul moved out), I can't help imagining water seeping in at the Olafsson house: along the utility line passageways into the basement, from the rain gutters, from the North Saskatchewan River, which has been rising all week in the June heat, engorging as the snow and glacial ice from high in the Continental Divide finally melts and comes plunging across central Alberta.

If I were still with Paul, I can imagine how he would have bridled. "You're becoming compulsive," he would have said. "Don't tell me you're thinking of going out there again tonight."

So what if I am? Isn't that precisely how I've managed to pull this project together?

At nine o'clock in the evening, when the light is still fine and bright, I drive once more to Olafsson House. I breathe deeply before I enter. The slightly rotting smell of damp wood hangs in the air. It was here this morning, and, I am sure, has always been here. Markus built the house in 1892, shortly after he left the Dakota Territory. Beneath all the Gothic surface decoration, the plaster wallboards, the latticework, the upper dormer, is only a disguised log cabin, its proportions strongly resembling a small seventeenth-century Swedish manor house.

As soon as I open the door to the cellar, I know what I'm about to see. A sour sewer-like odour pervades the air, much worse than this morning. At the bottom of the stairs, a film of water covers part of the floor.

Twelve days till opening.

I place another call to Kramer. I can't reach him, but I leave a message saying we still have a problem. He had better get someone down right away from the company responsible for the restoration work. I add the word "please," which I realize

I've sometimes been forgetting these days. Then I go back to the top of the stairs and tightly close the door to the cellar. The stench is giving me a headache.

On the way out, I pause in the study. It is not large, but the presence of a study in a farmhouse during that era was itself unusual. Sepia photos of Helga and the six children are displayed on the wooden desk: Einar, Siggi, Gudjon, Elin, Helgi, and Thomas. Oddly, the two boys who died in their adolescence are those who face the camera most bravely, Einar tall and thin, with a calm, bored demeanour, Siggi, the second eldest, blond, round faced, wearing a light smile on his face, as if teasing the photographer to catch it. A stained inkwell, an assortment of pens, pigeonholes stuffed with old copies of the Icelandic-Canadian papers from Winnipeg: Markus's lifeline. A bay window looks out on a hay meadow, the family cemetery, and the curve of the river.

I stand beneath Markus's portrait, above the desk in his study. The photograph was taken in 1911. By that time, he was acclaimed in both Europe and North America. He'd written five of his seven volumes of poetry, but he hadn't yet started his trilogy.

A square head. Stubborn chin. Close-trimmed moustache, thick grey hair like a brush, the veined complexion of the out-doorsman. But for his eyes, he could easily have been taken for the reeve of a rural municipality or the postmaster in a small town. The eyes are heavy-lidded, warm but full of sorrow.

This is where Markus worked, in the minutes and hours he could spare from his farm chores. Often he composed through the night while his wife and children slept. It's not so surprising that in Icelandic the verb *ao yrkja* means both to till the soil and to compose poetry.

As I lock up the house, I think bitterly about what Longman will say. That I was wrong from the beginning to champion this site.

"I do not quite understand," he said when we obtained initial funding, "precisely why the site cannot be moved to Heritage Village?" He used phrases like "better public access" and "infrastructure cost savings."

I tried to imagine looking out the window in Markus's study at some reconstructed drugstore from Wainwright or a restored Anglican Church manse, instead of the North Saskatchewan and its rushing water. "It would be wrong, totally wrong," I told him. "This house mustn't be separated from the river."

Sometimes Longman doesn't get it. I've explained to him several times that Markus credited the river as being his source of inspiration. The river divided him from the other West Icelanders. It provided him the geographical equivalent of the social isolation he required for his art. It helped him to go his own way.

"The North Saskatchewan River presented a serious obstacle that prevented Olafsson from fully participating in mainstream activity," Ena Ericson wrote in *Notable West Icelanders*.

Mainstream. Markus would have enjoyed that choice of phrase, he with his love of language, his passion for metaphor and imagery. I am no expert in these matters, of course; my purpose is to conserve as well as possible the physical artifacts that formed the foundation for Markus's remarkable life, and, to the best of my ability, present them in a coherent, intriguing manner to the public and scholars alike. If I do this properly, with heart, as it should be done, who knows what gates of discovery I could open for the Ericsons of this world?

More of Ericson's words from *Notable West Icelanders* slide into my head.

They accused Markus of godlessness.

He said he was just speaking his mind.

This was in Dakota Territory in 1888. Eight years earlier, his ideas had driven him there from the Icelandic community in Wisconsin.

The winter winds in Dakota picked up such velocity across the treeless plains that Markus had to attach safety ropes to walk from his house to his barn.

The response of the Icelandic community was equally chilly. Markus left the Lutheran Church when it wouldn't allow women to vote on congregational matters.

By 1885, a dry cycle hit. Dust storms carried off the seed the Icelandic farmers had so carefully planted. Grass fires, fanned by the strong winds, destroyed most of the remaining hay meadows and prairie.

Then the eastern millers of Minneapolis formed a monopoly to establish what the farmers thought was an unfair price for flour, and together with the American railways drove up transportation costs and drove down grain prices.

By 1889, Markus had had enough. He scouted land further west in the North-West Territories, in the parklands of what is now central Alberta. When he returned, he led his family and six other families further north, altogether a party of thirty-five men, women, and children.

They stopped near the settlement of Edmonton, by the North Saskatchewan River. Never had Markus seen such rich soil: heavy, black loam over clay subsoil. The few English settlers in the area grew potatoes as big as turnips. Tomatoes were untouched by frost until as late as September 12.

"I like the country south of the North Saskatchewan River," he wrote back to friends in the Dakota Territory. "The soil is rich and the grass abundant, with clumps of trees and fine fishing in the rivers and lakes. I believe the land is well suited to mixed farming, and the winters are said to be less harsh than those in Manitoba and Dakota."

For the first six years, he worked to break twenty-five acres of land. He built the first school in the district and defended women's rights. Later he championed the United Farmers of Alberta.

How intrigued I was to learn that the United Farmers were the first political party in the country to propose universal medical care! Nothing came of that proposal, of course, and by the time that party came to power, Markus had completely given up on organized politics.

I walk outside to the river's edge. On this side, the banks rise a couple of metres above the water. On the other side, they are ten times as high, thickly fringed with willows. Behind them, mostly hidden from sight, stand the houses built by some of the city's rich: dermatologists, corporate lawyers, long-departed hockey players. In the distance, the tops of the downtown high-rises reflect the last glints of sunlight. The High Level Bridge spans the river like a delicately forged black steel necklace.

Markus had built the house on a promontory where the river curves. Thanks partly to my lobbying, all twenty hectares have been declared an historic site, although it will be a year or two yet before the department gets around to renovating the sheds and replanting the garden. Even then, we'll be able to give only a general idea of what the homestead was like in Markus's time. The visitor must make the imaginative leap.

A few years ago, leafing through Markus's journals, I found a reference to another spring like this one. The spring of 1901. That year the snowfall in the Rockies reached record levels; the North Saskatchewan began rising early in June. By July it had nearly flooded its banks.

More of Markus's lines from "North Saskatchewan in Flood" come back to me:

Restless by night through all the hidden shadows,

You dream of old blue glaciers melting.
Winter's never finished until its waters find the sea.

Some believe Markus actually forbade the water to rise any more. They claim that he was what the Icelanders call a *kraftaskald:* a power poet. For centuries, Icelanders believed such poets could ward off evil with their verses, cure or cause an illness, create fortune or misfortune for others. Such a skill had been documented in his native country since ancient times.

I explained these aspects of Markus's life a few weeks ago to Carrie. "Our problem is," I said, "how do we get all of this across, without confusing the issue? It's his creativity we want to focus on. Probably it's best to just hit the main points and not get into all the 'citizen of the world' stuff."

I realize now that I didn't even give Carrie a chance to answer my question. Maybe Paul had a point. Maybe I am becoming as driven as this damn river.

When I get back to my house, I unroll Carrie's graphics. Something is troubling me, although I'm not exactly sure what. Certainly the panels are informative without being fact heavy. The sepia photos of Markus and Helga and their six children should make the family real enough to most visitors, even to children raised mostly on television images.

The pacifism business in the Olafsson panels is, I think, neatly encapsulated in a few sentences that tell of Markus's "enduring belief in human progress and rational thought, a belief that led him to obey his inner convictions over those of the state when Canada was drawn into the First World War."

He was drawn to Unitarianism, the panel explains, because of his belief that "individuals have the ability to distinguish between right and wrong."

But he never became a member. He always went his own way. That's the most important lesson I've learned from his life, and I only wish I'd learned it as a girl. Maybe Gretchen and I would still be friends.

I particularly instructed Carrie not to portray the Icelandic predilection for folklore and superstition. Markus was, if anything, a rationalist. Until recently, most of the histories published about Icelandic Canadians didn't mention that some believed in mythical spirits that inhabited the landscape, both here and in Iceland: the night trolls that froze into stone if caught by daylight; the *huldufólk* that inhabited lakes and other places, and whose dwelling place one must take care not to disturb for fear of their revenge; the wraiths or *svipur*, human likenesses said to appear to people before their deaths; and the walkers or *afturgöngur*, the spirits of those dead before their time, said to remain near their corpses until their natural lifespan had lapsed.

There's no record of such things among the artifacts we've retrieved from Markus's homestead, no physical evidence, for how could there be? The academics who study such phenomena know enough about these beliefs, so there's no need to give them more than a nod. For the public who visit the site, it will be enough to demonstrate and celebrate his own independence of thought.

For me, what is most important is the image of Markus in

his study on those June evenings, pen in hand, looking occasionally out his bay window into the night, writing new line after new line. Conquering the urge to watch the water rise, even when farmers further down the river, some in higher spots than this, evacuated their houses and took their sheep and cattle to higher ground. Always Markus battled the urge to follow the ways of those around him.

I'm certain the exhibit will succeed in making this point. Yet I am still vaguely troubled as I put the panels away.

In the night, I wake up shaking. The old dream again. I'm running as fast as I can on a gravel road, trying to catch up to Gretchen. When I'm close enough, I reach out for her, but there's nothing there. Her flesh dissolves into the air.

I throw off the cotton sheets with their design of dancing lilacs and pad over in bare feet to the tiny balcony off my second-floor bedroom. Three o'clock in the morning, and the sky already washing away to fragile blue and turquoise around the edges. The wide river valley below is darker than the sky. My eyes rest there. If I shared the beliefs of my ancestors, I would think the *huldufólk* were creeping out from under large rocks and setting out to capture my soul.

Markus rarely slept through the night, no matter the season. He welcomed the darkness, the way it clamped down on distractions and put an end to his farm labours. Perhaps that dark, barren volcanic island made night-worshippers of both of us.

I have sometimes wondered if his last, silent years could

possibly be explained by a brief reprieve from the insomnia that plagued him most of his life. His responsibilities on the homestead left little time for his creative pursuits during the day. Only during the night did he usually have time to write, although occasionally in his later years he asked his sons to take his place in the fields. Not doing his share made him feel guilty, however, so he rarely did this.

I sleep fitfully until seven o'clock, and resist calling Carrie until eight.

"Sorry to call so early," I tell her.

Something in the way she greets me makes me think she expected my call.

"I've been thinking about those panels," I tell her. "All that stuff about the wraiths and the *huldufólk* that I told you not to focus on? The stuff that was in the material I dropped off last night? Well, I think maybe we should include a brief mention of them, after all. I'll e-mail you some text."

"Oh good," Carrie says. "That should give us some strong visuals."

Just as we're saying goodbye, she asks why I changed my mind. "That Olafsson guy didn't believe in that stuff, did he?"

"No, not at all," I tell her. "But those beliefs were part of his people's past, even though a lot of Icelanders are a little embarrassed about them. They might have had some impact on Markus."

"I get it."

Despite lack of sleep, I feel better than I have for twenty-four hours. The day keeps on improving when Kramer calls to say that the restoration company will send someone out to Olafsson House at two o'clock. I'm even starting to look forward to dinner with Paul.

Monday Evening,
JULY 9, 1962

For years after that summer, I could not visualize Gretchen's face. I would imagine I was walking behind her, on a country road, and when she turned around to wait for me, her face blurred and became as featureless as a beaten egg. Each time I imagined her figure in front of me, I would hope that this time she would appear to me as I had known her. But she never did. Only old photographs brought her likeness back into my mind, the brown, serious eyes and the determined set of her chin, the expression that missed being pretty only because it was so grave. I haven't looked at those photos for years. I don't want to remember Gretchen's face, or anything more about that summer. I recall all too much without even trying, although I sometimes wonder if my memory is as sharp as I think it is.

My mother was the one to point out how closely Gretchen and I resembled each other. I didn't believe her. "You look like sisters," she observed. This was the fall after the last summer Gretchen and I spent together, when I stopped wanting to go to school and couldn't sleep at nights. The school counsellor thought it might help if we looked at old photos of Gretchen and me and talked about what had happened.

"It's the expression on your faces," my mother said. "You two look as if you couldn't say 'boo' without checking it out with each other."

I didn't believe her, because it hadn't occurred to me before that Gretchen might have needed me as much as I needed her. We were both treading in the dangerous waters of adolescence that summer, both out of our depth, and the difference between us was the way we tried to stay afloat. I never wanted to show Paul the photos, because to do so would have been to draw attention to the very worst side of my nature, a prevaricating, opportunistic side he had no idea existed. A side he surely could not have loved.

Another image that stays with me: the exact way my mother tossed her apron at me that afternoon when I came back from swimming lessons and said Mac wanted to see her. She had bacon spitting on the propane stove, and new potatoes on the boil, and wore the white nurses' shoes she favoured when her feet bothered her, which was often. They made a hollow sound when she stepped on the spot by the stove where the linoleum buckled.

"Here," she said, and threw the apron into the air. She'd never done such a thing before.

Without waiting to see if I'd caught it, she headed into the bunk room to freshen up.

It was not my mother's custom to wear makeup on the days

she wasn't expecting visitors. My father and I were used to seeing her go about the house with pink foam curlers in her hair all day if she had an engagement that evening. But when she went out, she always applied lipstick and loose powder, and coiled her nut-brown hair into smooth rolls which she sometimes tucked under a black net, sprinkled with velvet cut in the shape of tiny diamonds. The result was impressive. I knew the name for her kind of looks: not pretty or beautiful, but handsome.

It was only later that I wondered why my mother always presented two faces to the world, a plain one for my father and me, and a more glamorous one for others. I didn't stop to consider that I might be doing the same thing, serious and studious with Gretchen, pliable and frivolous with Rosemary and Arlene.

I caught the apron, but I didn't put it on. The apron was a full one, a cotton print of teapots and ivy leaves, with ruffles around the edges. I didn't care if I splattered fat on my T-shirt.

My mother was gone only for twenty minutes or so.

"You've got everything under control," she said. I'd set the table, remembering the paper serviettes and the chilled water glass my father demanded. He was the only person I knew who actually made a point of drinking six glasses of water a day, the way the Canada Food Guide said you were supposed to.

"I'll have to hustle," she said. "I need to drop into the office tonight. I'd like you to come with me, Thora."

"Okay."

I was surprised that she asked me, but then I remembered

that my father played cribbage with Uncle Gisli on Monday nights. I never thought for a moment that my mother might simply want my company. Which gives me a little rush of sadness when I think of it now.

The drive to Gilead took twelve minutes. On the way, four cars passed us. I recognized only one of them: Vivienne Krywulak's Chev. Both Rosemary and Arlene were in it. Vivienne waved as she went by.

"Is there a bingo tonight?" my mother asked. The Legion held bingos twice a week. We never went because the United Church considered bingo a form of gambling.

"I think bingo's Tuesday and Thursday," I said. "I don't even know if they have them in the summer."

The night was warm and fragrant. Cultivated fields on either side of the road – immense acreages of wheat and oats and barley – shone an almost fluorescent green. Although the fields were large, they were edged with windbreaks of caragana or spruce or poplar to protect them from the prevailing west winds. This landscape had a beauty of its own, although I missed the glistening bowl of the lake.

Four or five families owned most of the land between the lake and the town. Their forebears, in the last part of the nineteenth century, had been among the first settlers to break the soil in the area. The farmhouses near the road told their story: new ranch-style bungalows with big picture windows, often on a barren patch of ground; old cube-style wooden houses, paint peeling, behind caragana hedges further away from the road. The new casting away the old.

Within two years, the gravel road to the lake would be oiled, and a year later paved. The television antennas that sprouted from every roof would begin to draw in more than the regional station in Yorkton. Not far ahead, although none of us could see it, Canada's Minister of Agriculture would pay these farmers to leave their grain fields unplanted. By that time, another doctor would have taken Mac's place, and my parents would take care not to mention Gretchen's name in my presence.

When we reached Gilead, my mother turned up a side street to get to the hospital. If I'd been at the wheel, I would have driven up Main Street, which was usually deserted on weekday evenings, except in front of the beer parlour, or the town hall, if a special event was being held.

My mother preferred the residential streets. Mrs. Turnbull's rhododendrons were thriving, she said. The Petersons should cut down that tangle of old honeysuckles and start anew.

We drove past our own house, with its drapes drawn to keep the sun from fading the new broadloom carpet, and into the parking lot of the hospital. It was a rambling, two-storey stucco building with snappy green trim, an attached residence on one side, and the doctor's office on the other. I'd been born in this hospital in 1949, a year after it had been built.

I'd never before seen the hospital parking lot empty. Gilead

Union Hospital had not been designated as a site for emergency services during the strike, so the handful of patients left there when the strike was called had been transferred to the nearest hospital, in Teasdale.

"I guess Reg is the only person who's been here the last few days," my mother said. "Strange to think."

Reg was the hospital caretaker, a friendly man whose patient pruning resulted each spring in the most luxuriant lilac hedge in town. In fall, the mountain ash trees and ornamentals flamed with orange berries and maroon leaves, an extravagance of colour against the sky's hard blue brilliance.

We walked to the entrance to the doctor's office, on the left-hand side of the building. Inside, I caught the faint fumes of disinfectant. The linoleum floor was dark green, hard and shiny. The entrance opened onto a small receptionist's area, with a north-facing window. Against two walls, metal filing cabinets in yet another bilious shade of green gleamed with the look of military efficiency. The waiting room consisted of half a dozen straight-backed plastic chairs lined up against the wall that also formed part of the corridor leading to the examination rooms.

It was here that my mother worked part-time as a receptionist and medical secretary, happily conversing with patients, making appointments, and filling out hospital records. The other secretary, Mrs. Edgarton, a war bride who'd married a local farmer, was away on holidays in England.

I visited the office often during the school year, usually on my way home from school to ask for money for a soft drink or a comic book. I liked seeing my mother behind her desk. She always looked brisk and efficient, and invariably pleased to see me.

"I thought it would seem a bit creepy in here," my mother said. "It does, doesn't it?"

She walked toward one of the filing cabinets. "I'm probably being silly," she said. "But would you mind keeping an eye on the front door for a minute? In case anyone comes?"

I planted myself by the door. It was just before eight o'clock, and I could hear cars turning at the end of Main Street and driving back down. Doing U-ies, we called it. In a few years, that pastime would be banned by the town fathers, but by then I was gone and didn't care.

My mother opened one of the filing cabinets, the one I'd seen her go to when she searched for patients' records. She licked one finger and began leafing through them. In a minute, she retrieved a file.

She brought the file back to the desk and opened it.

"Want the light on?" I asked.

"No, no, this is fine."

Outside, the light was fading quickly. I thought I could hear voices in the distance, but I couldn't tell where they came from.

"Right," my mother said. She closed the file and put it in her purse.

I'd never known her to take home a patient's file before. Once, when my father was in for bronchitis, he asked if he could look at his own file, even though he said he knew he'd never be able to understand it.

My mother had refused. The files were confidential, she'd said. "Absolutely confidential."

Out in the parking lot, my mother cast a worried look back at the door.

"Isn't it funny?" she said. "It's as if there are ghosts around here."

"What did you take?" I asked.

"Nothing that concerns you, dear. Just some information that Mac needs."

I hated being called dear.

From somewhere near the centre of town came the sound of voices.

"What's that?" my mother asked.

"I don't know," I said. The voices arrived in varying pitches, the way a crowd sounds at sports events. But summer sports events were always held in the fairgrounds, and we could see from where we were standing that the bleachers were empty.

My mother turned out of the driveway and was about to go back the way we had come.

"Could we go down Main Street?" I asked. "To see what's going on?"

My mother pursed her lips, but her eyebrows lifted slightly. She always was curious. She drove halfway down Main Street, past Macleod's and the pool hall and the Co-op Store and the Post Office.

"What on earth?" she exclaimed.

All the angle parking spaces on either side of the street in front of the town hall were taken. Dozens of people crowded the entrance to the hall. I recognized a few faces – one of my teachers, a member of the choir, a few neighbours.

"Why don't you ask someone what's going on, Thora?" My mother stopped the car at the side of the street, behind some parked vehicles.

"All right."

I got out of the car. I wasn't used to seeing so many vehicles downtown, except when there was a wedding involving one of the big families in town, or the morning of the agricultural fair parade.

"Excuse me," I said to a large man who worked as a meat clerk in the Co-op Store. "Can you tell me what's happening at the hall?"

"Sure," he said. "It's a meeting of the Citizens' Safety Committee."

I went back to the car and stood on the street while my mother rolled down her window. "Them?" she said when I told her. "I'd never have believed they'd get so many people out."

I walked around to the passenger side of the Pontiac. People were beginning to crush their cigarette stubs out and move gradually back into the building. I thought how hot it must be in there on a night like this. Even in May, when Grade Twelve graduation was held in the hall, the place would heat up so much that it was taken for granted that one or two of the graduating class would faint before the ceremony concluded.

As I stepped into the car, I saw the Krywulak twins on the front step. Rosemary was smoking, and Arlene was patting her hair. They looked our way.

My mother, usually a maddeningly slow driver, accelerated so hard that the Orange Crush bottle I'd left on the floor of the car rolled right under the seat.

Cripes, why did she have to do that? I wondered if Rosemary and Arlene had seen us, and if they'd noticed any-thing unusual. My face tingled, the way it did when I'd been in the sun too long. I had the same feeling I'd had a year before, when some of the older teenagers had snickered as I walked through the hallway at school.

"Make a sound like a walnut," someone laughed that day.

Gretchen told me after school why they had tittered. Gilead had two grocery stores, a Co-op Store and Mike's Grocery, which was owned by Mike Ferada who was on town council. Most families shopped at one store or the other, and if something on their shopping list couldn't be found in one store, they simply went to the other. There were no conve-nience stores; the closest big supermarket was in Yorkton, more than an hour's drive away.

My mother and father and Aunt Stina and Uncle Gisli shopped exclusively at Mike's, because they said it was good to support independent businessmen. Uncle Gisli said the Co-op was socialist, which was the same as communist. I had never heard my parents describe it that way, although I could not recall ever seeing them shop in the Co-op. They shopped at

Mike's, I guessed, because they knew him and liked him.

According to Gretchen, a rumour was going around that when my mother couldn't find the walnuts she wanted at Mike's that morning, she'd made an awful fuss.

"They said she had a fit – that she absolutely had to have walnuts for some squares for the church or something," Gretchen said. "When the clerk said to try the Co-op, she said she'd never set foot in that store and never intended to, because it was communist. The clerk at Mike's had to go over to the Co-op herself and buy a package of walnuts for her."

"That's ridiculous," I said. "My mother would have just gone to the other store."

When I got home that day, my mother was at work and my father at the rink. The kitchen table was clear, except for a package of walnuts. When I saw those walnuts in their shiny package, the space around me seemed to grow and everything else seemed to shrink. I never had the courage to ask my mother about those walnuts, and after she came home that day, they were quickly put away or vanished into baking. Now I see that I was always wanting to leave things blurry; I feared the certainty of sharp lines and unassailable facts.

On the July evening after my mother and I visited the doctor's office, we drove back to the lake in silence. As soon as we reached the cabin, my mother walked over to the McConnells'. She told me not to expect her for a while, because after she saw Mac and Alexia she planned to drop over to Aunt Stina's for coffee.

I stayed alone that evening in the cabin, working on a miniature table and chair for the log cabin replica. Alexia and I planned to get together on Tuesday night to do more work on it.

I didn't think anything more about what I'd seen that night. When I worked on the miniatures, twisting pieces of wood the size of matchsticks into table legs or gluing layers of construction paper together to look like a Bible, my mind didn't stay in the present. It hovered back into the past, to the lives of my ancestors who had been among the first Europeans to settle this part of Saskatchewan.

Thinking about those people didn't make me tired and confused, the way I usually felt when I thought about most of the people I knew at Whitefish Lake or in Gilead. I recognized that learning more about those people who lived in the past would bring many surprises. But I also sensed that those surprises would never have the power to hurt or embarrass me, or make me feel different from everyone else, the way that surprises from people in the present could.

Tuesday Morning,
JULY 10, 1962

Gretchen stood at the edge of the water. The dog tag I'd traded with her flashed on her chest. She turned a pebble over in her hands. With her index finger she traced a circle on the surface. Her brow was mirror smooth and she wore a pleased look on her face.

Further down the beach, I dug my heels into the sand and waited for James Harrison to call the Advanced Intermediates into the water for our second day of swimming lessons. The sky was gauzy blue; the weatherman predicted a sizzler.

The others in our group splashed about in knee-deep water, wetting their thighs and abdomens and arms in the gradual way James said was best. I preferred a quick plunge.

Gretchen bit her lips – she might have been calculating a math problem. She looked up at the others in our group, and at the same time she rolled the pebble between her thin white palms as if it were the whole world and she could do with it what she pleased.

What did she see in that pebble? Perhaps the vestige of

some ancient sea creature? Eons ago, the entire province had been an inland sea. But in that one encompassing gaze I saw her take in the others in our class, and dismiss them, and although she couldn't have seen me from where she stood, I understood by the tilt of her chin that I was among those dismissed. I saw no hint of warmth in her expression, nor of curiosity, but something more unsettling: an obliviousness to everyone and everything outside the immediate focus of her curiosity.

I felt a lurch in my heart valves.

"Advanced Intermediates," James called out from the instructor's platform in the middle of the swimming area.

We began making our way towards him. Gretchen waited for me. She was smiling, and the look I'd seen on her face a few minutes before had disappeared. "Here come the mermaids," she said cheerfully. "Stay near to me, okay?"

During our lessons that day, we practised the side stroke. "Pickin' grapes," James called out. "You're picking grapes. Now reach for those grapes."

Next, a back float for relaxation. I found this easy. But Gretchen always started to sink.

"Straighten your back," I said. I stood beside her, blinking at the sun-spangled water. Everyone was assigned a swimming buddy and she was mine. She did as I said and squeezed her eyes tightly against the glare. But still her legs and torso began to sink. I couldn't understand why.

Gretchen didn't berate herself, as I would have done, saying things like: "I just can't get it" or "I'll never pass the test." Instead, she appeared fascinated by the phenomenon of her own failure. It made her curious about the reasons behind it, the same way she'd question why a *Camnula pellucida* had an unusual wing pattern.

"What we're dealing with here," she said, "is a matter of buoyancy. The question is, why am I having difficulty achieving it?"

"Less talking, girls," James called out. "Concentrate on your strokes. Everyone swim round the platform twice now. Side strokes. No touching the bottom."

I tried to stay near Gretchen, but I couldn't help edging in front. As I swam on the beach side of the instructor's platform, I could see the same groups on the sand as the day before: the Beginners mostly on one side, Seniors on the other, the empty blankets above both groups where the Advanced Intermediates staked their claim. By the second day of classes, we all knew our places. Arlene and Rosemary were in their usual spot, although that day Rosemary sat on a beach chair instead of sprawling out on a beach blanket as she usually did.

"Okay, not bad," James said. "You can stand up now."

He looked at his watch. We stood chest deep in the lake, gazing up at him as if he were John the Baptist. His legs were hairy and thin. He wore a thick green sweatshirt with kangaroo pockets where he kept his hands most of the time. He had an annoying habit of rubbing his knuckles, so that he often appeared in nervous motion. But he had a reputation as a good teacher. The students who took swimming classes at Whitefish Lake had one of the highest success rates in the provincial Red Cross swimming tests, which were held a week or two after classes ended. The examiners were usually from the city, Saskatoon or Regina, trim women with German accents or keen-eyed men with slight paunches who seemed to resent what the years had done to their swimmers' physiques. Frequently they took out this resentment on students, gleefully failing them for the slightest infraction.

James, however, told us we were lucky to have our examinations at the lake instead of in a city pool where the water was so clear the examiners could see what your arms and legs were doing every minute. A lake was more forgiving. It hid things.

"Okay," he said. "We're going to finish up with ten minutes of treading water. You'll have to do fifteen minutes to pass the test. Anyone need a quick review?"

"Yes, please," Gretchen said.

James summarized the technique: cup the hands, make large slow circles, stay upright, keep your back straight. Don't overtire yourself.

Billowing altocumulus clouds streaked across the blue sky. They formed wispy columns that reminded me of the floss candy my parents bought for me during the annual Agricultural Fair in Gilead. A light wind sprang up. Although the air wasn't cold, I shivered in my wet suit. I wished we would get moving. I rarely felt cold when I was immersed in the water, only when I was halfway in and half out.

"All right," James said. "I want you all to swim over to the buoys."

A line of red buoys floated at the outside boundary of the swimming area. The water out there was far above our heads.

"Do we have to go that deep?" I asked.

"You may as well get used to it," James said. "The examiner will take you out at least that far."

I looked at Gretchen. She smiled slightly and shrugged. The seven of us swam out together, staying close together. The water had turned dark blue and choppy.

When we reached the buoys, we formed a circle and began to tread water. One of our group, Bill McClymont, said his cousin had failed this part of the test because he froze with fear when he actually had to go out so deep.

"Trial by fire, you could call it," Gretchen said. "Or ice!"

James watched from a rowboat almost close enough to touch.

I kept expecting Gretchen to reach out for the boat. But she didn't. She kept up with the rest of us, treading water with regular kicks and strokes.

The water came up to my neck. I will not be afraid, I kept telling myself. I tried to think about how I'd felt diving into the deep water on Dominion Day, how the depths had beckoned me like a warm tunnel instead of frightening me. The water began to feel tepid, an enormous soft, wet cushion. I could trust the lake. All I had to do was kick my legs in slow, regular steps, like riding a bicycle under water, and make easy sculling motions with my hands, and I would stay safely and comfortably above the surface. Trust. Keeping afloat was all about trust.

After what seemed like half an hour, James called out: "Okay, come in now. Well done."

"My hands feel numb," Gretchen said.

"So do mine," said Bill.

Gretchen was quiet when we walked back up to our blankets to dry off. I was glad that she'd been able to tread water so well, but I was surprised too. The thought came to me that she could probably do anything if she wanted to. Maybe even break into Rosemary's circle.

On hot days, the instructors scheduled a free swim for thirty minutes after our lunch hour. By the time the Seniors finished their morning lessons, I was weak from the heat. The air smelled of baby oil and sweat and the wind-fresh scent of the lake.

When Ken Ponych blew the whistle signalling the free swim, almost everyone ran down to the water. He stayed up on the beach talking to Rosemary, who stayed in her chair. Of course we knew she couldn't get her bandages wet. James must have gone up to one of the picnic shelters to lay out the materials for more dryland rescue lessons after lunch, because I didn't see him anywhere.

Arlene was one of the first ones in the water, and she and some of the older teenagers started splashing each other in a far corner of the swimming area. Gretchen and I didn't pay much attention. The water felt cool and soothing. She plunged in quickly, as usual.

For a long time I have thought about what happened next. Was it because of the heat? Or did it have something to do with that wide sky? Did we watch others intently because the prairie landscape we inhabited was so open, so uncluttered, that it focused our attention on small grievances that might have gone unnoticed elsewhere? Were we unforgiving of any dark, inexplicable corners because our eyes had become accustomed to holding everything up for examination against that brilliant light?

Was there simply too little else to distract us?

An eaking excuses?

Gretchen was standing in waist-deep water with another pebble in her hand when the splashing started.

I heard them behind us, Arlene and her group, and then a torrent of water slapped my skin. I turned and saw five of the older teenagers approaching. They drove their palms against the water, sending anvil-shaped torrents into our faces, our ears, our eyes.

They probably would have stopped in a few minutes. Ganging up on victims on hot days was not unusual and seldom lasted long. All we had to do to escape was run up on the beach.

And then Gretchen threw the pebble.

I don't know who the pebble hit, or if it hit anyone. But as soon as it left her palm and arced against the sky Arlene yelled, and the group encircled us. They weren't slapping their palms against the water anymore. They were bending their knees and cupping their palms and aiming water as if in buckets in every direction.

We splashed back. So much water was being heaved and hurled that I could barely see who I was aiming at and which direction I was facing, and it seemed that everyone was turning on everyone else. I couldn't make out Gretchen's form from anyone else's. The whole sky shimmered like a thousand rainbows, and I saw Gretchen bobbing up and down in the water. She seemed to be smiling and laughing and splashing back.

And then I was splashing her too. Like everyone else. And like everyone else I was laughing and shouting. The sun felt warm, and the lake tilted into shining blue triangles. Crystal-like drops coated my eyelashes and every pore of my body.

How many minutes passed that way? I don't know. But then there was a different sound, a choking sound.

"Stop," I yelled.

But they didn't stop. They kept on.

I grabbed Gretchen and pulled her towards the beach. They only stopped then, and just for a second, and soon they were all splashing someone else in their group.

Gretchen coughed and coughed. Sometimes when I wake in the night, I still hear that rattling, hacking sound. "I'm okay," she said when we got back to our blanket. "It was all in fun."

I remembered the pebble and wondered if that qualified as fun. But I didn't dare mention it to Gretchen.

Tuesday Afternoon,
JULY 10, 1962

"We have to tell them," I heard my mother say as I came around the corner of our cabin that day after swimming lessons.

"I suppose," my father said. In his voice I heard the same defeated tone he used on the farm when he realized he couldn't weld a broken part and would have to go to town to order a replacement from the east.

My mother stirred cream into her coffee. She'd moved two wooden kitchen chairs onto the grass in front of the cabin, and set a metal TV table in between them. Slices of Icelandic cake, called *vineterta,* oatmeal cookies, and banana bread were laid out on the table, along with an opened envelope, my father's reading glasses, and the ever-present binoculars. We didn't have a patio, or patio furniture, either at the lake or in town, and I couldn't help thinking that the spartan settler stock in my parents never fully approved of the McConnells' plush striped lawn furniture and rainbow-coloured umbrellas.

Down the beach, Clement Hummel had started to take

kids waterskiing. Most days I would have been tearing down to join the queue, but my chest felt squeezed and raspy, as if I'd been the one who'd gotten water in my lungs.

My parents both looked surprised to see me. They'd expected me to stay at Gretchen's for a while after lessons, helping her with her hoppers or leaf collection, or taking a meandering walk over to the confectionery for ice cream bars or popsicles.

When I told my parents about how the older teenagers had ganged up on Gretchen and me in the water that day, they didn't say anything at first. One seemed to be waiting for the other to speak. My mother hummed. My father drummed his fingers on the TV table. He looked more tired than usual. I realized he hadn't been out in the boat for two days, since he'd towed Alexia back to shore.

Finally he said, more to my mother than to me: "I wouldn't have thought it. I just wouldn't have thought it."

"She's not quitting swimming lessons," I said.

"I wonder if that's wise, under the circumstances," my mother said.

This surprised me. My mother hated quitters. Once when I'd wanted to quit Canadian Girls in Training because they spent too much time singing and I couldn't hold a note, she'd said the most important thing was to stick to something once you'd made a commitment. She'd left the decision up to me. I'd decided not to quit, and started enjoying myself once we began making kites instead of singing hymns all the time.

"What's in the letter?" I asked.

Years before I was born, my father had smoked until he

developed severe bronchitis and had been ordered by a doctor to quit. Although he hadn't touched a cigarette since, he had a way of separating his right index and middle finger when he was nervous or stalling for time. That's what he did that day. His clipped fingernails clicked against the metal tabletop.

My mother held her coffee cup in both hands in front of her chest, studying it as if it were an offering. Out on the lake, I could hear Clement gunning his engine. It seemed a long way away.

"Thora," said my father, "have you heard anything more about the Citizens' Safety Committee? Anything at all?"

"A few times," I said.

"Who from?"

"Just kids on the beach. I don't know all of them."

"What did they say?" my mother asked. "You can tell us. I know children can be cruel sometimes."

She often said this: children can be cruel, things go in threes, the good you do comes back to you, no man can serve two masters. Little aphorisms that formed the posts and beams of her world.

"They were just talking about things that committee had done in other towns," I said.

"And nothing about here?"

"No." I had no wish to tell my parents anything but the truth. There was puzzlement in their eyes, and hope as well.

"So you haven't heard about anything more happening here, since the other night?"

I was about to tell them that Arlene Krywulak had wanted

me to spy on Mac, but my father appeared satisfied. I decided not to volunteer anything.

"Well, let us know if you hear anything," he said.

He turned to my mother.

"I didn't think so," he said.

I started to say something about Arlene, and then I stopped. I didn't want to make myself look bad. What would they think if I told them Arlene had been so sure I would tell on Mac? Better not to mention it.

My father reached for the envelope and placed it in his shirt pocket. It was only as my parents rose that they seemed to realize I was still there. The thought came to me that I had fulfilled my purpose and had disappeared for them, the way a medieval messenger was dismissed from court.

"What's the big deal about the envelope?" I asked.

My father looked at my mother. She was stacking the coffee mugs and humming. His eyes brightened. "Someone's been threatening the McConnells," he said. "And now, any friends of the McConnells, it seems."

He reached for the envelope and pulled out a page of white paper. I read the neat block printing:

To the McConnells and any other doctor lovers:

We want the doctor out of town in forty-eight hours or his family will be sorry. That goes for any doctor loving friends.

The Gilead Citizens' Safety Committee

"You mustn't say anything," my father said. "Not to anyone. Not even Gretchen."

"Where was the envelope?"

"Under the door when we came back from town," my father said.

The light had shifted on the lake. Pale aluminum bars ribboned the water as the sun tried to shine through billowing altocumulus clouds. Mothers were bringing small children up from the beach, going to their cabins to prepare dinner for husbands who would soon be driving in from Gilead or nearby farms. Their figures pulsed, the way images in the town's movie theatre sometimes did when the projectionist hadn't loaded the film properly. Nothing that I looked at seemed real to me, except for my parents.

The world had tilted.

"Aren't you even going to tell the McConnells?" I asked.

"What I'm going to do, right now, is tell the Mounties." He walked towards the Pontiac. "I'll be back in an hour, Mother," he said.

After dinner that night, I walked over to the McConnells', as planned, to work on the miniature with Alexia.

"Oh, good, you came," Alexia said. "Some manual therapy."

No one else was in the living room, but I could hear a radio softly playing upstairs in Mac's study. "Gretchen's deep in her categorization," Alexia said. "I promised I wouldn't disturb."

I followed her into the back porch. "How's this for starters?" she asked. "I did them up quickly so we could get going."

She handed me a sheaf of scale drawings that illustrated the floor plan and exterior of the Sigurdson homestead, with allowances for the windows and doors. She'd measured every detail – the height of the window, the door frame, the amount of space between the steps. For a moment, I felt the same way I did looking at physics texts for two grades beyond me, and then I began to see that every part was reduced by the same proportion.

"How did you get the measurements?" I asked.

"Oh, I took a quick drive out a couple of days ago," Alexia said. "And I've done this before, you know."

Used razor blades covered on one edge with tape gleamed on the work table, as well as a pair of long-nosed pliers, a small mitre box, a rat-tail file and a 12-inch flat file with cutting edges, a divider, and compass.

"It's quite easy, really," Alexia said. She gave me the measurements and I set to work with a handsaw. The twigs Alexia had selected were sturdy and straight. The air filled with the fresh, sweet smell of new wood. I liked the feel of the saw, the speed at which it sliced through the wood.

We worked steadily for the next hour and a half or so, sawing, cutting, measuring. By the end of the evening, we'd produced all the basic pieces, made allowances for the windows and door and the wood stove in the middle of the kitchen, and applied the flooring.

I looked at the little structure, with its floor the size of a handkerchief and the little twigs fashioned into logs, and I thought there was bravery in it. Even if it was small and humble, it was being created with care and correctness and proportion, and it sprang from our own hands and imagination. I'd remember that buoyant feeling later, and the sensation I had that you could create a world with your hands, not just your head, the way that Gretchen did.

Alexia nodded, as if in response to my wordless appreciation. "I think it's going to be good," she said.

An RCMP car, black with yellow trim, pulled up as I was leaving. Uncle Gisli's Cadillac followed behind it. He parked in Mac's driveway, careful not to block the police car. Aunt Stina and my parents were with him.

"We'll see you in a few minutes," my mother said to me. "Off you go, then."

I remember that I began walking back to the cabin, but stopped when I was beyond the shadow of the flagpole. Alexia was calling my name.

Tuesday Evening,
JULY 10, 1962

What puzzled me that July was how things that had been so familiar to me – the lake and the beach and the people I had known for years – might at any moment·shift and reshape themselves. The surfaces stayed the same, but down deep unsettling transformations had occurred, the same way teenage girls may look unchanged after menstruating for the first time, while inside their organs are becoming those of women.

As I opened the door to the McConnells' cabin, I heard one of the Mounties saying that "a person couldn't be too careful." The two Mounties sat around a table with the McConnells and my parents. They stopped speaking for a moment when I came in.

Alexia poured cocoa for Gretchen and me, coffee for everyone else. I noticed again, when she handed me my cup, how she'd cut her nails straight across and used clear polish. All the moons on her nails showed, the cuticles were pink and healthy, not ragged like mine.

The strike would be short, Alexia predicted.

An amicable agreement would soon be reached, Mac concurred. He leaned back in his chair as he said this, his ever-present cigarette as usual burning precarious amounts of ash. I knew that Alexia sometimes said he should cut down on smoking, but he always replied that there was no proven link between lung cancer and smoking, and besides, he needed to relax somehow.

No doubt the hospital would reopen in a few days, Mac said. Previous patients would come back. Nothing much would change, except that if the government won out, doctors would need to fill out more forms and send them to the Saskatchewan Medical Care Insurance Commission instead of getting paid directly by their patients. The Commission would then issue cheques to doctors for payment.

The black night pressed in against the windows. Usually the McConnells' cabin seemed airy to me, but that night it was hot and sticky. Thousands of insects clustered on the other side of the panes, straining to reach the source of light through the glass. Smoke wafted above our heads; one of the Mounties lit a cigarillo. My mother raised an eyebrow in a barely perceptible movement. The evening took on a suspended feeling, and for a moment I imagined that the cabin was actually a miniature and the blackness on the other side of the windows was really the pupil of a giant's eye peering at us.

"If the College wins," Mac went on, "most of the doctors I know will call it a triumph for individual freedom. And yet they've basically taken away my freedom to practise medicine right now."

My father looked surprised. "Seems to me," he said, "the government's got no business telling doctors how to run their business. Not any more than telling farmers." He glanced at Gisli. "That's why we're going down to Regina. To give Lloyd and his boys that message."

"That's right," Uncle Gisli said. "This isn't the Soviet Union."

When we left the McConnells that night, the four adults huddled for a few minutes. My father advised Mac not to allow Gretchen to continue with the swimming lessons.

But when we left, Gretchen asked me to pick her up the next day as usual.

"You sure?" I asked.

"Of course."

I awoke to shuffling sounds.

They came from somewhere outside the cabin. A woman's voice. No, two women. Two sets of footsteps on the grass.

I thought I heard a heaving sound. A sob? A gasp? I couldn't tell.

Below me in the lower berth came the sound of my father's light snoring.

I was the only one awake. I stayed rigid in my bed, half afraid of what I might see if I crawled over to the window at the end of my bunk.

Knuckles knocking on Dr. McConnell's screen door. The gentle sound of the aluminum door opening and closing.

A girl's voice, tight and trembling.

Rosemary's.

And then Arlene's.

Wednesday Morning,
JULY 11, 1962

Morning came, cool and white and calm, the surface of the lake a gleam of pewter. From the double bunk beneath me rose the steady, rhythmic sound of my parents' breathing. I climbed down, dressed quickly in the tiny changing room, then unlatched the front door and stepped outside. The air had a bite in it, and the sky was neither white nor blue nor grey, but an indeterminate gauzy opal that refused to hint at what the day might hold.

Tiptoeing back into the cabin, I took a paring knife from a kitchen drawer and walked across the road to the ditch. My runners sank into the soft muck at the bottom, but I pulled myself up on the other side by grasping at the red willows that grew in thick clumps amidst the huckleberry and rose bushes.

Patches of milky sky backlit the encircling green-leaf filigree. Many of the branches appeared too gnarled or irregular for my purposes, but a few possessed the pleasing conformity I sought. Some of these desirable branches peeled easily away from the parent stem. Others clung stubbornly, and these I had to slice off with my knife, using vigorous see-saw motions.

As I walked back to our cabin, I noticed that Vivienne Krywulak's car wasn't in her driveway. She usually left for work at seven-thirty.

It was only seven o'clock.

For an hour or so, until my parents arose, I sat on the cabin stoop and peeled bark off the delicate, evenly shaped twigs. I took great care to remove every shred. The greenish-yellow heartwood smelled damp and wild, like fresh-turned earth and spring rain. The surface was cold satin against my fingertips.

When I finished the peeling, I braided the twigs into chains. Alexia would be pleased, I thought. We'd gleaned the idea for willow braids from a book on pioneer crafts she found in the branch library in Gilead. The book was from the United States, but Alexia said that in Western Canada we had to use whatever resources we could find, just like the early homesteaders. The glossy coloured photographs illustrated the wood-carved ornaments that settlers had used to beautify their homes, employing whatever materials they had at hand, from chalices carved from bull horns to willow braids twisted into garlands and wreaths and picture frames.

The braids were easily made, the captions claimed. The trick was to select young stems and to fashion them into shape immediately after detaching them from the parent branches, while they were still moist and pliant. By the time my parents were up, I'd made half a dozen tiny wreaths and garland braids.

"Look," I said. I held them up to the light. "They're for the miniature."

"That's something different, isn't it?" my mother said.

She walked softly that morning in hand-knitted slippers. My father's shoulders at the breakfast table appeared more rounded than I'd remembered seeing them. I thought about the note he'd received and about the RCMP corporal saying you couldn't be too careful, and I wondered what else had been said at the McConnells' the night before.

When my mother had finished her cereal, she picked up the paring knife I'd left on the table, wiped off the bits of bark and gum from the blade, and plunged it into the enamel dishpan to wash with the breakfast dishes.

"Did you hear anything during the night?" I asked.

My parents both shook their heads.

"I thought I heard something at the McConnells'," I said. "But maybe it was a dream."

"What did you hear?" my father asked.

"Sounds. Voices." I didn't say anything more. I didn't want to upset them.

"Maybe you could put up a few posters around the beach?" my mother asked me that morning before I went to lessons. "Richard brought over a bundle yesterday."

Richard was the publisher of the *Gilead Review,* and, like Uncle Gisli, also a member of the Gilead Chamber of Commerce.

My mother often asked me to put up posters for her various volunteer efforts, hospital auxiliary sales, the Icelandic

Ladies Aid tea and plant sale, the United Church Women's fowl supper. I liked the feel of a sheaf of posters under my arm, a small box of tacks in one hand, and the responsibility of deciding on the best telephone pole or fence or doorway on which to display my notices.

But when my mother made her suggestion that morning about putting posters up at the beach, my stomach tightened.

"Okay," I'd said.

I hadn't taken any of the posters to the beach. I'd waited until my parents drove off. They were going to spend the day in town, helping Uncle Gisli and Aunt Stina and other members of the Keep Our Doctors Committee with preparations for the Regina rally. After they left, I stuffed the posters under my mattress in the bunk room.

"Can I show these to Alexia?"

I was at the McConnells' door. In one hand I held my beach bag and in the other the willow braids.

"She's not here right now," Gretchen said. She had red shorts pulled over a blue-and-white swimsuit. I thought she looked like the Union Jack.

"Then can I put these with the miniature cabin?"

"All right."

I darted into the back porch. The miniature stood where we'd left it. Alexia had sanded some of the surfaces and fitted in casement windows. Looking at the tiny structure, I could imagine people moving inside, living their lives in another time, and I felt a power I had never experienced before. Those people existed, in my mind anyway, because Alexia and I had made a place for them. If anything were to happen to that place, I reasoned that they would also cease to exist. I would have lost the only friends I had who didn't demand too much of me. Unlike Gretchen, I was not an imaginative child. I needed the props of reality to feed the dreams in my head, not the silly dreams about tulle net gowns and gold watches, but the dreams that mattered.

I laid the braids carefully down on the table and went back to Gretchen. "I thought I heard some sounds from your place last night," I said. We started down to the edge of the water, on our way to swimming lessons.

"Did you?"

"I thought so."

"Well," Gretchen said, "you might have. But I'm not supposed to say anything." She was looking at her feet as she spoke, watching for flat stones to skip. She was the only girl I knew who could skip stones better than the boys on the beach. She said it was because she understood the physics.

I hoped that Gretchen would say more, but I knew that as a doctor's daughter, she had to keep many secrets from me. She couldn't help overhearing her parents discuss which high school student had become pregnant, which farmer was dying from emphysema, whose grandmother was about to be sent to the nuthouse in North Battleford. I considered these secrets wasted on Gretchen, whose interest in grasshoppers and wave frequencies and constellations far outweighed her interest in the people of Gilead.

That day, I tried to snap a hard shell over my curiosity. I didn't want to give Gretchen the pleasure of withholding information. At the same time, I envied Gretchen's detachment. How much bother I would save myself if I cared only about things that could be measured, like the size of grasshopper wings or the daily spread of leaf mould.

"This is a beauty," Gretchen said. She picked up a hard flat stone, white as alabaster, and tossed it hard across the water. It skipped eight times.

"You try," she said. But I didn't. What was the use? I knew I'd never be able to skip a stone as well as Gretchen. I had no understanding of physics, which seemed to be about things you couldn't see or touch or feel in your heart.

When Gretchen and I reached the public beach that morning, I could see right away that attendance at lessons was down. Gretchen said it was because the stores in Gilead would be closed the next day for the rally in Regina.

James Harrison must have noticed, because he addressed all the groups on the beach that morning. "We only have eight days of lessons left," he said. "If you're serious about passing your test, you'll be here every single day."

Only four or five Seniors were in their usual places on the right-hand side of the beach. I didn't see either Rosemary or Arlene. But later that morning, after our group had come in from lessons, Arlene went back into the water. She spoke with

James Harrison, nodded, and began a slow, strong Australian crawl.

"That's excellent," I heard James call.

I thought of asking Gretchen where she thought Rosemary might be, but I didn't. I was afraid to, because I could hear her answering silence before I framed the question. What was worse, I imagined that I could hear her satisfaction in depriving me, as she deprived the hoppers of oxygen in her killing jar.

At dryland rescue practice that afternoon, James reviewed life-saving equipment and demonstrated how to throw safety lines. I'd seen it all before, so I didn't need to pay attention. Instead I watched Arlene still practising her crawl. She swam harder and faster than I'd seen her swim before, and she didn't allow enough time for gliding, the way you were supposed to. Her hands didn't enter the water in the smooth, cupped way they usually did. Sometimes they splashed the surface like a beginner's.

I thought of what James said about how humans are one of the most versatile of all creatures in the water because of the great variety of positions, manoeuvres, and directions we can assume. "It's all thanks to a set of ball-and-socket joints in our shoulders and hips," James had told us. "We can do it all, seal dives, alligator rolls, muskrat swims, porpoise swims."

Gretchen had told me once that humans probably started to swim for economic reasons, groping for food in muddy shallows. She'd described the Nimrod Gallery in the British

Museum, where bas-reliefs depicted Assyrian swimming fig-urines from about 800 BC. I could tell by the way she spoke of those reliefs that she was more interested in the *idea* of swim-ming than in actual swimming, and I blamed all the facts and ideas and opinions in her head for weighing her down. Maybe that was why she couldn't swim as intuitively as I could, or as hard and long and fast as Arlene.

James gave each of us a turn at tossing the plastic lifebuoy towards Bill McClymont, who pretended to be a drowning victim. The key to a good rescue, James said, was to know exactly where your safety equipment was, and to learn to act so automatically that you didn't have to think about what you did. He demonstrated how to coil the rope, then place one foot at the end of it, and swing the lifebuoy attached to the other end several times before tossing it high in the air.

The first time I threw the rope, it didn't uncoil properly. Some of the coils were irregular and caught on others, tan-gling the rope. "Try again, Thora," James said. "Watch that tendency to be careless."

The second time I threw the buoy, it landed within a few inches of Bill.

"Terrific," James said. "Now your turn, Gretchen."

Gretchen held the rope stiffly with her chunky white arms and when she tried to swing, her face turned serious and she seemed to be thinking hard. She managed to toss the lifebuoy only a few feet.

"Put a little more power into it," James said. She didn't do much better on her second and third tries. Her physics weren't doing her any good here.

"Bill, I guess you've drowned," James laughed. He looked at his watch. "That's it for today. We'll work on this again tomorrow. Everybody going to be here?"

He looked at me.

I nodded.

"That's good," he said, warm voiced. "I was hoping I wasn't going to lose any of you to the rally. Arlene says your parents are going for sure, to support the doctors."

My face went red.

"I actually don't know if my parents are going," I lied. "Or which side they're on."

Gretchen was behind me, coiling the rope from the last throw. But after I spoke, I heard the rope drop on the sand and turned to see her walking away without a word.

I helped James finish the coiling. When I went back to the beach blanket, Gretchen was gone. I looked down the shoreline and saw her chunky figure walking alone in the distance. Every once in a while, she stopped to fling a stone into the water.

There were whitecaps on the lake now, although it had been calm earlier. The waves that slapped the beach were already heavy with sand.

Saturday Afternoon,
JUNE 20, 1998

At two o'clock, a few minutes after I arrive at the Olafsson house, a young man drives up in a yellow truck and introduces himself as Tom Bittner from the consulting company in charge of site restoration and design. He wears clean pressed blue jeans and an Eddie Bauer shirt. From the way he carries himself, arms swinging and a glow on his freshly shaved face, I can tell he's not expecting to find any problems he can't solve. Kramer and I lead him down into the basement. It's danker than I remember. The level of water has risen another two centimetres in the last hour; Kramer says the pump isn't working properly and can't keep up.

"Christ," says Bittner. He returns to his truck for high boots, descends the stairs and steps into black liquid. He flashes his lamp against the walls.

"I'll have to poke around a bit," he says. "But first we better see about that pump."

He and Kramer work together for a few minutes, but the motor continues to misfire and run slowly. "I've got a bigger unit in the truck," Bittner says, and half an hour later the new pump is installed.

I fight back the idea that the leaking is just a symptom for something else, that you can't remake the past and that Markus's house is about to cave in on its foundations. The thought of opening day, less than two weeks away, presses in. I hear hundreds of pairs of feet on the floors above, imagine the wooden floors splitting and splintering and all the visitors plunging into cold, black depths. Their arms flail. Their voices shriek. Their mouths and nostrils plug with black gritty water; they struggle for oxygen.

Kramer and I follow Bittner outside where he gets a long tubular device. It's a probe, a fancy hearing aid, he says. If you put your ear to the top, it will magnify many times the sound of any water running several metres below the surface. Rather like a stethoscope for the earth's arteries.

He starts at one corner of the yard, listens for a moment, then moves a few metres west. I sit on the stoop and try to tame my thoughts. The grass in the yard is coming along nicely with all the spring rains. It's a mix of wildflowers and weeds and hayseed, which will be scythed later in the summer, as Markus's sons used to do.

Watching Bittner's figure cross the lawn, I think about all the different ways the people I know look at the earth beneath our feet. For Bittner, the earth seems to be a medium for underground channels and streams that can be scientifically charted and analyzed with sophisticated sensing devices. For Paul, it is a band of stratified layers of earth and rock to be probed ever more deeply. For me, the earth is a tracing paper that reveals where human beings leave their footsteps in time, even though those are often no more than a humble fragment of a cooking pot or a projectile point or a used cartridge. All of us looking down, not up, for our answers. All of us placing our faith in what can be measured, heard, seen, counted, touched.

Bittner crosses over to the small woodshed beside the house, then proceeds further past the family cemetery and back to the hayfield that we seeded for the first time this spring. Some of the shine has worn off his face. He keeps placing the water detection device to his ear, staring at it as if he can't believe what he's hearing, and then moving it to a different position.

Establishing a grid. Of course. That's what he must be doing. It's no more mysterious than that.

In a few minutes, Bittner is back. The sky has turned tank grey and the wind is up.

"Find out anything?" I ask.

He shrugs and purses his lips. "I eliminated some things, is all. Whatever the problem is, it's not your usual groundwater accumulation. There's no problem with the rain gutters or the grading or the piping. But you're getting major inflow into the southwest corner from somewhere."

"Any idea why?"

"No. I'll do a few more tests."

He thinks he'll have some answers by Sunday.

"Call me as soon as you find out anything," I tell him.

The day has been so exhausting that I consider calling Paul to cancel dinner. It's as if the water in the basement is seeping away at the energy I need for the opening.

But first I call Longman. He answers on the second ring. I picture him in a leather chair in the study of his Riverbend house, a patrician sight with his silvered beard and ratty tweed jacket. I know what he'll imply – that he was right all along. That Heritage Village is on higher ground. That we should never have insisted on rebuilding on the original site.

"Bad news," I tell him. "We've got serious seepage problems at the site."

He whistles. "How bad?"

"Don't know yet. We might have to delay the opening. At the worst – well, I don't want to think about the worst."

I tell him that we should have more news on Sunday.

"I'll meet you down there tomorrow," he says.

I feel a rush of gratitude that he would do this for me. Sunday afternoons are usually reserved for his painting classes.

"I'm not sure if I should mention this now, Thora," he adds, "but I had a call from Svava Erlendson. She'd heard some rumours about problems at the site. One of the donors is getting edgy."

"Damn. Let's hope we find out what the trouble is soon."

"We will," Longman says, in his usual optimistic way.

He told me once that the work we do in our department is as important as any written histories. If we can replicate at least a few of the structures that our predecessors lived in, he said, and if we can allow others to experience the breadth and depth of these physical parameters, we'll be closer to under-standing them – and therefore ourselves – than if we read a dozen texts.

Not that the texts aren't important, he'd said. "But these days, what do you think the chances are that many people are going to read the texts? Any texts?"

My head is starting to ache again. All I would need would be for the Friends Society to pull out some of its funding. The department, through the historical foundation, is investing fifty per cent of the capital costs for Olafsson House, but without the Friends Society behind it, the interpretive pro-grams would have to be drastically cut. Markus's homestead could become just another monument.

My head feels clearer when I'm in my car and climbing out of the river valley. "The North Saskatchewan River could be rising to levels not seen since 1901," the radio broadcaster says, then starts a long explanation of how heavy the snowpack in the Rockies has been this winter. I switch stations.

Poplar fluff blows lightly in the breeze as I drive past Heritage Village, where a refurbished steam passenger train whistles at a refurbished station, ready to give rides to cultural tourists. All I can see of the village from here are the roofs – house roofs, store roofs, church roofs. Each of those roofs ren-ovated or restored or refurbished. All of them relocated. All of them out of place.

I drove this road for the first time in 1974, with a copy of an old topo map from the 1940s on the other seat of my Volkswagen Beetle. A red circle marked the spot where I expected to find Markus's Alberta homestead. The road hugged the bank, following a bend of the river that created a wide peninsula on the south side.

The Land Titles Office hadn't been much help. The property belonged to the city now, the clerk had said, and yes, there were a few old buildings on the site, but he couldn't tell me much more. No one seemed interested. Edmonton was in the midst of the oil boom then, cranes everywhere, new office towers going up each month, old buildings destroyed before your eyes. No one cared about an old house once owned by an Icelandic-Canadian poet most people had never heard of. That's when I contacted Longman at the Historic Sites Branch and heard about the opening for an historical archaeologist at the provincial museum.

I felt a lurch of disappointment in my chest when the ramshackle buildings came into view, and I realized from the map that this must be the Olafsson homestead. Two small sheds leaned at gravity-defying angles, along with the remains of an outhouse and the decaying skeleton of a two-storey wood-frame house. From a bird's-eye view, the house would have appeared to be nearly framed by water. The river's restless movement animated the air.

I sensed bravery in the placement of the homestead, and faith too. No other settlers had dared to homestead here. The homestead must be preserved, dammit, and I'd be the natural one to do it.

As I leave Heritage Village behind, it occurs to me that I may have become so accustomed to winning battles that I barely acknowledge the slightest possibility of failure any more. Like Gretchen, I'm sure I understand all the physics involved here. Between us, Longman and I have been aggressive, perhaps too aggressive, some would say, although I try not to listen to that kind of backbiting. Think of it: more than a dozen historic sites established in Alberta since 1974, everything from a bison jump at Fort Macleod to a working coal mine at Drumheller. An "entire network of the physical history of the province's migration patterns," as one newspaper columnist termed it.

And the Olafsson house will be the jewel in the crown. I don't mean that it will be the largest or the most elaborate. What I mean is that Markus's life illustrates, in my view, a stirring example of the wisdom of following your own path, however isolated.

Jewel in the crown? Christ. Knock it off, Thora, I tell myself as enter my office. Stop taking yourself so seriously. That was one of the things Paul was good at, stopping me from becoming too earnest and self-important. I'd better keep the dinner date.

Still, I can't help but be proud of some of my achievements in preserving the past. The tiny fur trading fort in the northeast burned down years before we got there. We spent two summers figuring out where the foundations had been laid, and another year sifting and probing before we could begin to piece together any decent human story. Then we tackled other minor outposts in the Peace Country, an Oblate mission and a house that belonged to a clerk of the Hudson's Bay Company.

The most recent poster on my office wall is also the largest: an artist's concept of the Olafsson House, circa 1920. The year of Markus's death. "I want it," I told Paul the day I found out from Longman that the Olafsson homestead site had been declared an official Alberta historic site, with funding earmarked for a major restoration. I called him from up in the Peace Country, where I was still finishing up last details on an outpost there.

"Oh boy," he said. "This will only encourage you."

I spend the rest of the afternoon completing the computerized donor list: a leather horse harness from A. Keller; a maple sewing machine from Ulla Kolbinson; a Rawleigh's linament bottle from Jack Mahan; a brass spitoon, Anna O'Brien. As usual, I become so engrossed in my work that I lose track of time.

Carrie calls late in the day to say that she'll drop off a concept for the new interpretive panel at my house tonight.

"Good work," I tell her. At least something's starting to click.

"It's cool stuff," she says. "God, Iceland sounds like the end of the earth."

"During the Dark Ages, the Catholic world viewed Iceland as the gateway to hell," I tell her. I learned this from Markus's letters the autumn after that awful summer, just as I learned that the first known volcanic eruption occurred there in the year 894, only twenty years after the island was settled. That was when Katla exploded from beneath the Myrdals Jökull, a glacier, in the south part of the country. Waves of ice and lava swept over the tiny settlement, pushing everything out to sea. To this day, the area is desolate and uninhabitable.

Of course, Markus scoffed at the Catholic idea of hell. He called it ridiculous, he who always resisted authority, whether in the form of the church or the state or the hateful Norwegian or Danish monarchy. "The reality should certainly be enough for a reasonable person to form his own conclusions," he wrote. Ever the rationalist.

Yet he couldn't resist describing those terrible infernos, and his words enthralled me. Imagine a country the size of Virginia, he wrote, but add more than one hundred volcanoes, dozens of them active, more than twenty-five steaming vents, and thousands of craters and lava streams that choked thousands of acres of farmland.

When was the exact moment that Markus gave up on the struggle to create a better life in Iceland, and instead looked west across the ocean? I could find nothing in his letters to tell me. But all his life he remembered the strangling fumes and the dark clouds, heavy with ash, and the way the ground shook and icy meltwater exploded from the glaciers, adding flash floods to the horror of the red-hot lava streams.

"It's much better there now," I assure Carrie. "But yes, the Icelanders certainly endured a lot of hardship."

As my sandals slap along the museum's tiled floor on the way out, I think of that young girl who blocked my way the day before, the one with the woolly hair and the tittering laugh. She wore a white T-shirt and ultra-baggy blue jeans with a hole in the knee. When I was that age, we wore them as tight as our skin. All of us except Gretchen, who never wore jeans. She said the reason why she didn't like them was because everybody else did.

It occurs to me that I never would have found my own path without Gretchen, and I never had the chance to thank her.

Wednesday Afternoon,
JULY 11, 1962

Being thirteen is like standing on the soft ridge of sand that divides the shallows from the deep water. Beneath your toes you can feel the grains of sand sink beneath your weight and pull you forward into cool, dark waters.

You want to be pulled in.

And you don't.

That July I kept being pulled forward and forcing myself back. And then, the afternoon before the rally, I returned alone from swimming lessons to find the door to our cabin slightly ajar.

We rarely locked the door at the lake except at night. Mosquitoes and flies were the intruders we most feared. Still, it was unusual for my parents to leave the door open for more than a few minutes. And since the conversation with the Mounties the evening before, a cord of anxiety seemed to be tightening around us. My father hadn't even left his change on the kitchen table overnight, as he usually did.

The driveway was empty. My mother and father were still in town helping out with preparations for the Regina rally.

The miniature was the first thing I saw when I pushed open the door to my parents' cabin. Someone had brought it over to our cabin from the McConnells'. It was set on a plywood sheet on the kitchen table.

What was left of it, that is.

The roof that Alexia and I had carefully built two nights before had been completely smashed in. All four walls lay in splinters. The glass from the casement windows, specially ordered for Alexia from Vermont, had disintegrated into shards. The graceful veranda had been hacked beyond recognition. Only the frame of the little structure was recognizable, although it tilted badly to one side.

The sight was as astonishing and horrible to me as if a dozen invisible lake monsters had crept up the beach and gone berserk, each attacking the miniature from a different angle, each trying to be more vicious than the others.

The room seemed to shrink, the walls contracted around me. A picture came into my mind of Gretchen coiling the rope at the beach, of how my lying words to James must have sounded in her ears, and how she must have heard them with every step she took back to West Beach and every stone she skipped. I could see her reaching for the hatchet Mac kept for chopping firewood. Walking quietly into the porch when her mother was out. Bringing the blade down. Furiously.

I knocked and knocked at the McConnells' screen door, but no one came. The flag was down, signalling that Mac was away, but I could hear a radio on inside.

Down the lake, children were gathering wood for a camp-fire that night. Part of me wanted to dash down the beach and throw what was left of the miniature into their pile of twigs and branches and other rubble. Another part – a stubborn, unexpected part I hadn't known was there – fought the impulse. It was as if a cold metal bar had lodged in my stomach, keeping me from bending or falling. I wasn't angry anymore, or rather, I was more than angry.

I placed the wreckage of the miniature on the steps of the McConnells' cabin and ran down to the water. I dove into the shallows and swam underwater for a long, long time, fol-lowing the ridge that dropped down into deep water. I sur-faced only briefly, glad each time to return to that other world below. The water was greyer than usual, still mixed with mud particles stirred up by heavy wave action the night before. When I opened my eyes, I couldn't see my outstretched hands, but I kept on swimming anyway. I was weary of the light above the surface, the light of a Saskatchewan summer that bounced from the endless prairie sky and reflected in the shining lake, endless, all-encompassing light that glowed even under cloud cover. It seemed to me a false light, illuminating nothing, although giving the appearance of doing so. A mocking, trickster light that burned my eyes and made my head ache.

I wanted to float forever in a shadowy world of ash-greys and charcoals.

When I emerged, the Pontiac was back and my mother was in the kitchen making lemon meringue pie.

A stillness inhabited the place inside me that previously housed anger. But it wasn't a calming stillness, like the way the wind dropped over the lake at twilight. It felt more like the still centre of a whirlwind.

I didn't say anything to my parents about the destruction of the miniature. I was not the kind of child who liked to go to her parents with troubles and defeats, only with triumphs.

Shortly after supper, it began to rain. My parents and I played hearts for a while, and listened to the nine o'clock news on the radio. The announcer said that businesses in at least forty Saskatchewan communities, including the two major cities, had agreed to shut their doors the next day to allow both employees and employers to support the Keep Our Doctors Committee cavalcade to Regina.

"Did you manage to put any of the posters up, dear?" my mother asked, handing me a cup of cocoa.

"A few," I said. Another lie.

At ten o'clock we all went to bed.

I lay awake for a long time, listening to the waves.

As I was falling asleep, I remembered what Susan Mellers had said about Gretchen a few months before. This was after a science exhibit Gretchen had entered in the regionals in Yorkton had been damaged by a careless truck driver. I knew she'd worked on the display for about two months.

Some kids in the back of the class tittered when our teacher told her the news. Gretchen had shrugged and said, *"C'est la vie."* She'd never mentioned the incident again.

Susan passed me a note. "Nothing ever ruffles her feathers, does it?" she'd written.

Lying there in my bunk, I caught the blurry outlines of another emotion mixed in with my sorrow and anger, a smug satisfaction that made me ashamed and giddy at the same time. I'd ruffled Gretchen McConnell's feathers.

Saturday Evening,
JUNE 20, 1998

Paul is already halfway through an appetizer by the time I make it to the restaurant, twenty minutes late. Sceppa's Trattoria on 101st Street is an old favourite, perhaps because nothing seems to change there. Still in the same unpretentious basement location on a gritty part of Edmonton's north side, still the same green-checked table-cloths, the same schlocky testimonials from hockey greats on the walls, the same chairs with their chipped paint, the same sensible cafeteria style. "No fancy frills," states the sign at the entrance. "Our aim is good food."

"Sorry," I start to say. Paul waves away my apology.

"No problem," he says. "I know this is a hectic time."

I force myself to meet his gaze. The archaeologist in me has long made a habit of trying to unearth the depths under people's appearances and not be surprised to find the worst, but in Paul's case I've rarely found anything but amiable good nature. Which makes my actions of our last night together even more reprehensible.

"I can't believe we've been behaving like this," he says. He shakes his head and smiles slightly. It's a private smile, the way you smile at yourself when you've done something really dumb, like tripped on your own shoelaces or put the coffee pot in the fridge.

"I'm a little surprised you'd keep calling," I tell him.

Paul tells me about the downtown hotel where he's been staying, about how strange it is to shop alone, about how he's taken up competitive badminton at the Royal Glenora. I talk about some of the problems at the site, and as I do, I can feel some of the tension that's been in my shoulders the last weeks start to ease.

We met three years ago at a career development workshop for high school students. We had both been asked to appear on a panel to talk about our career choices. When I arrived, Paul was sitting at the end of the panelists' table, looking at topo maps on his laptop. I thought I recognized someone who was almost as much of a loner as I'd become.

During the panel discussion, I explained that I had become interested in archaeology in the fall of 1962, when my uncle cleaned his attic and found a box of letters from an Alberta farmer who was also an Icelandic poet. There were one hundred and twenty-three letters, I explained, all written by Markus Olafsson to his cousin, Kristjan Sigurdsson, my great-grandfather. The two friends arrived in Canada from Iceland on the *SS St Patrick* in 1874 and survived a dreadful winter in Kinmount, Ontario. Then they split up. The letters spanned forty-five years, from the time the two separated in 1875 to Markus's death in 1920.

"I'd had a tough summer," I told the students. "Somehow finding those letters made the difference. My father translated them for me, and I just became passionate about learning more."

Later, when the moderator asked us to sum up our advice to students, I wanted to tell them to follow their hearts. But that sounded too earnest. "Examine your obsessions," I suggested. "They'll give you clues."

"The word that works better for me is 'engagement,'" Paul said. "Think about what most engages you. Assuming it's legal, of course," he laughed.

Later we sat together for lunch. The menu included corn on the cob, and I remember thinking it strange that he didn't put salt on his corn.

"The rebel in me," Paul said. He had the grace to smile. We learned that we were both divorced, both had some free time on our hands, both had an interest in the past. Paul's interest, though, extended mainly to the geological: Quaternary, Tertiary, Cretaceous. When we used to go for long walks in the North Saskatchewan River Valley, his eyes darted to the exposed bedrock strata of the north bank, with their layers of sandstone and coal and shale. My eyes were at my feet, watching for flakes or projectile points from early Native camps.

We're nearly finished the main course when Paul assumes the embattled look that he often wears on his way to a meeting with a particularly difficult client.

"Any chance for another try?" he asks. I feel my face

starting to burn. I'm thankful that Paul has chosen a public place for this discussion. A large family is squeezed around the table behind us, celebrating a birthday. Their joyous shrieks seem to pierce right into my eardrum. I look out the window for a moment, at a back-alley view of stucco and clapboard houses.

"I don't know," I tell him. "I was so horrible to you." I can't help but remember that for six weeks this spring I promised to go over the book proposal Paul had drafted for the provincial geological society. But I just didn't get around to it. There was so much to do at the Olafsson site.

"You were angry," he says. "Understandably."

"Still."

"Look, I don't care if you never show me those albums. I was out of line."

I explain that I can't stay late. I still need to look at Carrie's graphics tonight, so she has a chance to fine-tune them before Tuesday.

"Maybe we could go for a walk tomorrow?" Paul says.

"I'll probably be at the site for part of the afternoon."

"Call me when you're free," he says.

I can't seem to bring myself to nod, but I don't shake my head either.

The new graphics are in my mailbox when I return home. They make my blood chill. Carrie has juxtaposed two portions of Ericson's text with charcoal drawings of blasting volcanoes, superimposed with carcasses of dying sheep and cattle. I read from the first panel.

Slaughter winters.

That was the name the Icelanders gave to the worst of their winters, seasons so cruel that drifting Polar ice masses sometimes crushed hard against the coastline, almost encircling the island in their clasp. Few hay meadows survived the unseasonable temperatures, spring storms, and summer blizzards. Farmers killed cattle by the thousands rather than see them starve. It was said that polar bears roamed the country, carried there on platforms of ice from their Arctic homeland.

During the most severe winters, tens of thousands of people either starved or were poisoned from eating rotting carrion. Those that lived survived any way they could: stealing, killing, boiling up gruel from seaweed and lichen and fish bones, eating ravens and foxes. Sometimes the famines lasted ten years. In parts of the country, the aged and helpless were killed and pushed over cliffs.

The people made blood sacrifices to try to ward off the unrelenting cold, but the hardships continued: Torture Winter, they called the winter of 1602-03. Year of Misery, 1604-05. Horsekiller, 1696. Waterless, 1697. Blood Winter, 1821-22.

The second panel shows spewing lava streams, burning meadows and barren fields. I read on:

The worst thing about the eruptions was what happened later. This is a frequent theme in Olafsson's poetry. In fact, it has been posited that he never came to terms with the after-effects and that his lifelong insomnia can be traced to these early traumas.

The danger of the eruptions was not limited to lava streams and spewing, glowing rocks and icy deluges. It also came from the airborne pollutants and poisons brewed deep within the volcano's belly.

"Sometimes, a few months after an eruption, farmers would notice that their hay meadows were growing particularly well," Olafsson explained in a letter to the editor that appeared in the *Heimskringla,* an Icelandic paper published in Winnipeg. "Then, weeks or months afterward, their delight would turn to rage. When the hay grew high, it took only a warm day to set the meadows ablaze, so laden were they with sulphur and phosphorus and other gases."

Olafsson was replying to a letter in the previous issue, from a farmer discouraged by his attempts to make a living farming in Western Canada. Olafsson never brooked such complaints; he said progress was only won by hard work. He displayed little pity for those who, failing as farmers, blamed external factors.

The burning hay meadows weren't the only devastation to be endured. A year, perhaps two, after an eruption, local farmers would begin to notice that the leg bones of some of the cattle and sheep were sticking

out on their backs, under their stomachs. Genetics
gone wild beneath their loose hides. Tumours big as
melons sprouted on their skeletal frames. In the worst
cases, open sores developed, flesh rotted away, and the
tails of afflicted animals dropped off.

It was said that if humans drank the same water,
their flesh would also peel away.

When I'd first read Markus's descriptions of this phenomenon in his letters, I began to have nightmares about my
bones rearranging themselves in hideous ways. The dreams
frightened me, but less so than my recurring dream of Gretchen.

The worst thing about the eruptions was what happened later.
I walk into the spare room, the one Paul used as his study.
From a high cupboard I take down a childhood photo album
from the years 1960 to 1962. I haven't looked at it for years.

Plunge in, plunge in. It's something I've been forgetting to
do lately. I try to force myself to open the first page of the
album, but instead I hold it on my lap for a long time. My
palms start to sweat and my forehead feels squeezed by a tight
band. After a long time I return the album, unopened, to the
high cupboard.

How would someone writing about my pathetic history
describe the summer of 1962, I wonder. Blood summer?

Thursday,
JULY 12, 1962

It hailed the night before the Regina rally. The crop report that morning carried news of patchy but extensive damage throughout the Yorkton district of east-central Saskatchewan. We slept through it all.

By eight o'clock, my parents, rested and cheerful, waved me goodbye. "We might not be back till late," my mother said. She wore a print dress that day, black jersey with pink roses, short sleeves, a Peter Pan collar, a string of pinkish pearls, and matching earrings. Being in a car with her would have been like traveling with a rose garden.

My parents planned to meet the others in the Gilead cavalcade at the schoolyard at eight-thirty that morning. From there they would drive for three hours to the prairie capital, partly on windshield-cracking gravel roads that cut southwest across rolling parklands, dipped down into the Qu'Appelle Valley, and reached their destination on the pancake flatness south of the valley.

I wondered what it would be like to accompany my parents. I was relieved that no one had made that suggestion. Politics was the business of adults, along with income tax and mill rates and grain subsidies.

I shut the door on the empty cabin and walked barefoot down to the edge of the lake. Pockmarks from the hail had drilled the sand with dark indentations. The silky lake reflected back the soft white glow of the sky, and the air felt warmer than it had for days.

Vivienne Krywulak's car, and Dr. McConnell's, were still missing from their respective driveways.

Only two or three boats bobbed in the water out at Peter's Point. According to Uncle Gisli, the Keep Our Doctors Committees had organized cavalcades from all the surrounding towns, "although whether we've done better than those SOB Citizens' Safety jokesters has yet to be seen," he'd told my father the night before. He'd come over to show my father an article in the Regina *Leader-Post,* which quoted the third-ranking official of North America's 850,000 Shriners. The man, the imperial chief rabban of the Zem Zem Temple in Erie, Pennsylvania, had told Toronto Shriners that the Saskatchewan government was an unwitting accomplice in a Communist plot to overthrow the western world. Probably there was not one Communist in the Saskatchewan government, the chief rabban had said, but "subtle propaganda had undermined the fabric of society."

"There are a lot of Shriners in this province," Uncle Gisli told my father. "I'm estimating we'll have about thirty thousand folks turning up in Regina tomorrow. Whaddya bet we'll bury socialized medicine by the end of the month?"

My father had nodded, but declined to bet.

I did not stop that morning to pick up Gretchen for swimming lessons. As I walked along the water's edge to the public beach, however, an urge came over me several times to turn around and see if she was following me. Each time, I resisted.

About halfway there, I noticed an odd-shaped bit of flotsam that must have been tossed up on the beach the night before. The object was small, white, circular, and fluted around the edges. I bent down to pick it up, but stopped, recognizing it as the remains of one of the cupcake candles Gretchen and I had set out on the lake on Dominion Day. I left it where it was, half hidden by seaweed.

Odd, I thought, that out of all the candles we had lit that night, only that one had reappeared on the beach. There wasn't anything special about it that I could see, and yet it had survived the waves and the winds to return to its place of origin, when most of the others were probably at the bottom of the lake. Why had that one stayed afloat? Had we applied the wax to the bottom of that cup with extra care? Or perhaps with *less* care, slopping the wax on so thickly we'd made it unsinkable?

When I reached the public beach, Gretchen was already there, reading *A Girl of the Limberlost*. She did not look up. I laid out my own beach towel several yards down from hers, near Bill McClymont. He wore an earphone attached to a transistor radio in the shape of a plastic rocket.

"Anything new?" I asked.

He took out the earphone.

"They say there's two thousand people going to Regina this morning, just from Saskatoon."

"Which side?"

"They don't know."

Bill's parents taught at Gilead Composite High School. They always shopped at the Co-op store, so I hadn't been surprised to see them in front of the hall the night the safety committee held its meeting in town.

Arlene sat cross-legged on a blanket on the Seniors' part of the beach, with Ken Ponych and a few others. She looked as if she had been crying. The group had a small transistor propped beside a beach bag. I couldn't see Rosemary anywhere.

"I should be there," I heard Arlene say. "I should be with my sister. But she said she'd kill me if I didn't go ahead and take my test."

"Don't think about that right now," someone else said. "I'm sure she's going to be fine."

I remembered overhearing someone at the beach the day before saying that Rosemary's leg hadn't been healing well, but I hadn't thought anything more about it at the time. And that day, on the beach, I had a lot of other things to think about. Up by the school buses, airwave voices from the radio blended with those of the school bus drivers and the rustle of wind in the poplars.

I longed for James to call us into the water. I dreaded it too.

After the whistle blew, I entered the water alone, behind Bill McClymont, Melvin Koschuk, and Orest Zankiw. I knew Gretchen was behind me, but I wouldn't turn around. Our morning routine each day was to begin our lessons by swimming around the instructors' platform four or five times, practising basic strokes in water that was about six feet deep on the far side. We were supposed to swim near our buddy and keep him or her in view. Buddies looked out for each other. That was the reason for having buddies.

Only when we were all up to our waists did Gretchen catch up to me. She touched my shoulder lightly with one hand.

When I turned, she held up both palms to me. She'd braided her copper hair that morning and twisted it into coils that made her look even more serious than usual. Her brown eyes were bright and alert. Her shoulders appeared ever so slightly caved in.

She said nothing.

I waited. And still she said nothing.

I remember the shock when I realized that she was not going to say anything more. The damage we had done to each other, those upturned palms assumed, was regrettable, but our natures would surely be pliant enough to forgive. We would go on as before.

Bill and some of the others had started the practice loops.

I couldn't bear the silence between Gretchen and me any longer. I didn't want to stand alone. And yet I kept seeing that pathetic little miniature, the roof smashed in and the splintered wood everywhere.

"Okay," I said. "We'd better get going."

"Okay," she said.

The lake water resisted my body. During the underwater pull of my front crawl, I kept making the mistake of reaching across the invisible centre line. My kicks were far too shallow, but I couldn't summon the strength to kick deeper, and I found myself breathing at the wrong point of the stroke cycle. A blustery, erratic wind had come up, frilling the water into sharp triangles.

The instant James blew the whistle for the class to end, my feet sought the security of the lake bottom.

It had been a long, tough morning, but as we walked up the beach for lunch, the last clouds disappeared and the wind dropped. Gretchen moved her blanket beside mine. We ate Cheez Whiz sandwiches and washed them down with cream sodas, watching the comings and goings on the beach. Once in a while, I thought about the cavalcade going to Regina, and how hot and sticky it would be in those cars, and how glad I was to be at the lake, breathing in water-cooled air.

"It's nice here today," Gretchen said. "I like it this way, uncrowded."

I nodded, although the beach had an abandoned atmosphere that made me uneasy.

"Holy cow," Bill McClymont yelped. He was listening to the radio again with his earphones. He pounded one fist into the sand.

"What is it?" I asked.

"It's a disaster for your side," he said. He frowned in concentration for another minute, not looking at us, before pulling out the earphones.

I hated the way he said "your side." That summer it seemed that everyone was always making assumptions about what side I was on, and I didn't feel as if I belonged on anyone's side. I was like those cupcake candles, going wherever the wind and the water took me.

Cheers went up from the circle where Arlene sat.

"What happened?" I asked.

"Only about five thousand people showed up," he said. "And only one-third of them were for the Keep Our Doctors Committee. All the rest backed socialized medicine. The doctors lost and the little guy won."

This seemed impossible. What about the merchants in surrounding towns that Uncle Gisli had called, his list of all the chambers of commerce across our region of the province, with neat check marks beside almost every one, stating they'd be at the rally to lodge their protest?

Bill was laughing again. "The guy said Premier Lloyd only watched the demonstration for a few minutes and then said there's 'quiet, solid' support for medicare. They're appointing a mediator – some Brit – to end the strike."

I looked at Gretchen, but she had gone back to her book.

How did the other news that afternoon originate? I can't be sure. Few people had telephones at the lake in those days, except for Mac and the people who ran the confectionery on the beach. Perhaps the news came from Jerry Embury, who often drove to the Dairy Queen halfway between the lake and Gilead for a hamburger, although he wasn't supposed to use the school bus for personal reasons. The woman there might have been in Gilead that morning and heard the news from someone in town. Or perhaps it came from one of the women working at the confectionery, who'd driven in from Gilead? Or from one of the parents, who'd dropped by the beach with a forgotten sandwich or pin money for a son or daughter?

What I do remember is that the news deluged the beach like a rogue wave.

Susan was the one who told Gretchen and me. We saw her at the confectionery where we went to buy ice cream bars.

"Did you hear?" Susan asked. "Rosemary Krywulak's had her leg amputated. It happened this morning. Arlene just found out."

Gretchen and I looked at Susan without speaking.

"The operation was in Saskatoon. Apparently the gangrene was so bad the skin under Rosemary's bandages was rotting. Yuck. It makes me sick just to think about it. All because her mother wouldn't let her go to a doctor in time."

"Because her mother's an idiot," said Gretchen.

"Is it true?" I asked Gretchen. "About the amputation?"

"How would I know?" she asked. "Rosemary's in Saskatoon, that's all I know. Dad heard there was an ambulance trip."

Gretchen walked back to her blanket.

I licked at my ice cream. I knew that relatives often had to wait for hours to know what was happening to family members when they went to the big hospitals in Saskatoon. It didn't surprise me that Arlene might just now be hearing the news.

The sun was so hot the chocolate coating on my ice cream was starting to thin. A few drops fell on my stomach and my feet. I remember hoping that Gretchen would save me the stick from her ice cream bar.

"Couldn't Dr. McConnell help?" I asked.

"Apparently he refused," Susan whispered. "So Vivienne drove Rosemary to Teasdale, and the only doctor there – the one who replaced Dr. Sullivan – was out on another emergency call. So Vivienne had to drive Rosemary all the way to Saskatoon."

My half-damp bathing suit felt slimy. Big puffs of fair-weather cumulus clouds tracked across the sky, well separated, flat on the bottom and rounded on top.

"Are you sure?"

"That's what everybody says."

"I'm sure that's not true," I started to say.

But Susan had already moved away.

James blew the whistle. The free swim period had started.

A breeze picked up sand and blew it into my eyes and ears and hair.

"Come on," I said to Gretchen. She put her book down reluctantly.

"All right," she said. "I have to admit, I'm baking."

When we walked by Arlene's group, everyone seemed to be talking at once. They were speaking in such loud voices that at first I couldn't make out what anyone was saying, but maybe that was because I was afraid to know. I thought I heard someone say "it's the truth" and then Arlene saying she was going to try to make a collect call to Saskatoon from the confectionery.

I tried not to think about Rosemary, but her image kept coming into my mind. I could see her on a hospital bed, and I imagined a surgeon's saw neatly detaching her leg. The thought of having only one leg was too awful to contemplate. How would things have gone so wrong so quickly? I saw her jiving with me in the school basement a few months before, the charms on her bracelet a gold blur. She'd never dance like that again. I shoved the thought away.

In the water, the red buoys that separated the open lake from the swimming area bobbed merrily. Some of the smaller children were in the shallows, laughing and scooping up sand. I wanted to get away from all the voices and immerse myself in the deep cool water of Whitefish Lake.

"Let's go out to the buoys," I said to Gretchen.

"All right," she agreed, as I'd known she would. She never could bear the idea that I might be able to go further or faster than she could. I started a slow crawl out to the buoys. James was watching the junior kids. He didn't notice as we slipped by.

"Here goes," I said, and dove under the surface. Down I went, and further down, where the depths were green and cool. I was a fish, an eel, a creature of another element, no longer battened down by gravity. Free and flying. When I surfaced, I was almost at the buoys. Gretchen was several yards behind me. I noticed a dead spot in the cycle of her alternating arm motion. She needed a lot more practice.

"The crawl always fags me out," she said.

I waited at the buoys, half expecting her to turn back. But she didn't. She kept gamely swimming towards me. Her torso rocked back and forth, because her forward strokes weren't straight, and I could see that her kicks weren't perpendicular and had little power of propulsion. I was tiring her out. Still she swam on.

"There," she said, touching the buoy.

I could tell that she wanted me to say "well done," but I didn't. I just nodded and began swimming to shore. I didn't look back.

Gretchen must have kept up with me most of the way, though, because when I got back into the shallows, there she was, smiling and flushed. We floated with our hands on the bottom, giving little kicks to move forward. The water was warm as a bath. I don't remember how long we floated, but it must have been long enough for Arlene to have made the collect phone call to Saskatoon and to have confirmed the news about Rosemary. If I hadn't been floating and dreaming in the shallows, I might have seen or heard her running back across the beach from the confectionery. Would anything have been different?

And then Arlene was upon us. Pushing and splashing and

screaming. Some of the others behind her joined in.

It was like the time before, I thought, and then I stepped back and saw that I might be wrong.

Maybe it wasn't like the time before.

They weren't aiming at me. They were aiming at Gretchen.

She shrieked and turned over on her side and tried to stand up and splash back. The water was only as deep as her knees. But Arlene stood astride her, hurling water and sand into her face.

I started splashing too. I didn't want to be left out of the chaos. I couldn't be sure if I was aiming at Arlene or Gretchen.

Gretchen started coughing, and then her back buckled and she kept on coughing. I caught the silver flash of the dog tag pendant around her neck. Her hand went to her throat. Her face started to turn white.

"Thora," she called. "Help."

"A sand shampoo!" Arlene's voice. "This kid should have a sand shampoo she never forgets."

"Underwater!" Someone else's voice. Who?

Gretchen being pushed underwater in the shallows, her hair fanning around her, her lips puckered, the veins on her throat becoming prominent.

Pushing. Shoving. Splashing.

"Doctor's brat!" Arlene again.

And then Gretchen again struggling to rise, her hair dark with sand, her forehead streaked, her eyes closed, fighting to get away, heading further away from the shore and the splashing crowd, toward the diving platform.

Everyone turning away from Gretchen, including me, pulled by the direction everyone else was going in. Finding another victim: Bill McClymont. But this time the splashing wasn't so hard. There was no pushing, no underwater sand shampoo.

The lifeguard's whistle blowing. "Cool it, kids," James yelled.

How long did the rest of us play in the water before I looked up for Gretchen? Certainly two minutes. Maybe more. I couldn't see her on the beach, or in the water, or on the diving platform. I walked away from the others, peering at the water, hand on forehead to reduce the glare.

Finally I called James. When I explained where I'd last seen Gretchen, he immediately dove into the water and swam toward the diving platform.

Seconds passed. Maybe minutes. And then he surfaced, clutching Gretchen's white, inert body. Blood oozed from a gash on her scalp. She must have swum under the platform to escape and then hit her head trying to surface. By that time she must have been exhausted, already half-drowned.

James carried Gretchen to the beach, turned her on her back, as he'd shown us dozens of times, pinched her nose, opened her mouth and started to give her artificial respiration, stopping only to tell someone to "call the ambulance from Gilead."

Susan ran up the beach to make the call. I stayed beside Gretchen. Saliva dribbled down her chin. Once in a while I thought her toes twitched. She wasn't wearing the dog tag any more.

I don't know how long James worked. We stood in a circle

and watched. The sun was hot and I didn't have a hat. My bathing suit dried completely and still we stood there. The chocolate stains on my suit stood out in the glare.

An ambulance wailed. None of this could be real, I thought. I had the sensation of floating, but then I felt the sand under my toenails and the sweat around my nape and the hum of transistor radios in the background. I yearned to be in a cool, dark place, somewhere else in time. Any time, except this present moment.

Two ambulance attendants ran towards us down the beach. James shook his head and looked up. "You kids better go," he said.

"Doctor's kid," someone yelled as Gretchen was carried on a stretcher to the waiting ambulance. "Serve you right if you never walked again either."

I looked up to see where the taunt came from. Arlene Krywulak. She stood momentarily in the doorway of the changing room a few yards away, then disappeared within.

Her words hung in the air. But it wasn't only Arlene's voice I heard on that sun-spilled sorrowful afternoon, for in her envious and vindictive taunt I detected echoes of another's voice, one I knew only too well.

My own.

Sunday Afternoon,
JULY 15, 1962

I n the midsummer heat, the back of my thighs stuck to the varnished wood of the pew in Gilead United Church.

It was three days after the drowning. My mother, to my left, looked up the hymns listed in the service and marked their places with torn-off strips of pink tissue. The hymn books were old, the bindings reglued and taped each spring by a committee of United Church Women. My mother's fingers lingered – sorrowfully, I imagined – over thin spots on the cloth cover.

To my right, my father bent his head forward to Aunt Stina. Every few minutes, my aunt would turn and look back to see who else had come. The scent of her Yardley Old Roses talcum powder wafted overheard. I imagined the particles being drawn in through my nostrils, hurtling down my windpipe until they latched onto the air cells in my lungs like greedy ticks that wouldn't let go.

You could choke on a lot of different things.

I turned around, pretending to pat some dandruff off my

shoulder. The back pews were jammed. At least twenty people, including Ken Ponych, stood near the doorway at the back of the church. I saw Vivienne Krywulak and Arlene three pews behind. No one had seen her since Gretchen's accident.

The closed walnut coffin, four pews in front of where I sat, glowed a buttery gold. I shut my eyes for a moment, then opened them. My heart clenched and I could feel a reverberation on my brow and wrists. Outside, the sun shone and the leaves on the Manitoba maples beside the manse quivered in a light breeze.

The fact that Gretchen's body lay within the coffin held no reality for me. I stared at the bright brass handles and fittings as if they would dissolve at any minute, half expecting to find myself sitting upright in my bunk at the lake, awakened from a bad dream by the night wind shaking my window.

I gazed up at the ceiling and wondered where the minister kept the latch key to the door leading to the steeple. Gretchen would have known. We'd planned to sneak up there one day and ring the bell. The bell had been donated years ago by an anonymous donor and hadn't been rung for years, after someone from another congregation had complained to town council that the morning bells woke him up while he was sleeping in on Sunday mornings.

I fastened my thoughts on that steeple, and what it would have been like to have climbed up there with Gretchen and rung those bells. And I began to build a box in my head. In that box I decided I would place all the thoughts I would ever have about the things that Gretchen and I had done, or would have done. And then I'd lock that box and never open it again. I'd silence those voices, the way the church bell had been silenced.

The organist, who was also the postmistress at the next town west of Gilead, began to play "Rock of Ages." We all rose.

It was only when Alexia and Mac walked to their places in the front mourner's row that my dream cracked. What was happening was real. Gretchen was dead.

The familiar firmness had disappeared from Alexia's stride. She wore a black silk sheath and turban with a pink rose at her throat. Lines were visible on her neck and around her mouth. Mac's black hair seemed more grizzled than usual. He kept his eyes down for a long time before he looked up at the casket. Gretchen's grandmother and grandfather were there from Montreal. Her grandmother, in a tailored houndstooth jacket, looked fresher than most of the townswomen in their floral print dresses or short-sleeved shirtwaists.

I don't remember much of the service, except that Reverend Cleland, whose forehead glistened with perspiration, said that we should grieve long and deeply. We shouldn't run away from our grief or deny it, he said. My mother wrote down some of his words, because she said they were so apt. "Grieve patiently, fully, honestly," the minister urged. "The only way to become whole again is to face what life brings." Those sentences still stick in the grooves of my brain, because once in awhile my mother read them back to me. I knew she wanted me to think about what those words meant, but somehow I could never bring myself to do so, not even when I grew up.

In the receiving line after the service, Alexia brushed her cheek to mine and held it there for several seconds. Mac clasped both my hands. If they said anything to me, I have long forgotten the words.

The United Church Women served coffee and refreshments after the funeral on the lawn of the adjacent manse. I saw Susan Mellers there, and Bill McClymont, and other classmates, but I stuck close to my parents. I felt as bruised as the fallen crabapples under my feet.

Part of me wanted to retreat. The other part wanted someone to ask me again what had happened. There would be a coroner's inquest and the police were investigating. "It was an accident," my mother kept repeating to everyone who called. "A horrible, horrible accident, started by that bullying Krywulak girl. And Thora got caught in the middle of it and didn't notice where Gretchen had gone. Of course, it was terrible what happened to the other Krywulak girl too, losing her leg."

"Do have at least one," Mrs. Kimball from the Macleod's Store said. She held out a plate heaped high with date squares and nanaimo bars and macaroons and gingersnaps. I chose a macaroon. I liked the deceptive brittleness of the surface against my tongue and the surprising way I could shatter it completely with the merest effort.

"Well, well," Uncle Gisli said to my father, "what do you think the chances are for getting back to normal after this?"

My father gave his familiar half-smile. "It'll take a while," he said.

The day after the rally, the Saskatchewan government invited British Labour Peer Lord Taylor to the province to help solve the medicare crisis. The Regina *Leader-Post* said in an editorial that Lord Taylor had helped found Britain's state medical plan and was "a leading Socialist in England."

Uncle Gisli looked over at Mac, who appeared to be in deep conversation with Reverend Cleland. "We're going to lose Mac, whatever way it goes," he said. "You watch."

Wednesday Morning,
AUGUST 22, 1962

D r. Percy Rose shone a light into my eyes once more, stepped back and rubbed one of his thumbs against the other.

His gaze wavered somewhere between the examination table and the metal chair where my mother sat, her back straight and ankles crossed. She might have been a model for a school poster on posture.

I did not know what to think of this new British doctor. His name struck me as faintly ridiculous. He had a tentativeness in his manner that I'd never witnessed in any of my visits to Mac.

"How long did you say this has been going on?" he asked at length.

"For three or four weeks," my mother said. "It's not so bad now, during the holidays. But it won't do when school starts. She needs her sleep."

It was the third week in August. The strike had been over since July 23, after the Saskatchewan government had agreed to let doctors opt out of the medicare insurance plan if they wanted.

"Well," Dr. Rose said, addressing my mother, "there's nothing physically wrong with her."

He looked at me. "Try to get some exercise. But don't worry about it too much. These things usually pass soon enough. She's had a shock, of course."

"All right," my mother said. She pursed her mouth. I could tell she'd been expecting more – pills perhaps, that would allow me to sleep through the night.

Maybe even a pat on the shoulder, as Mac would have done.

Dr. Rose stood at the door. "Well, then," he said. "Bring her back in six weeks if there's been no improvement."

On the drive from Gilead back to Whitefish Lake, I rolled the window down on my side and inhaled the faint smoky fragrance of late summer. The wheat fields shone.

"They'll be leaving today," my mother said.

She didn't have to say who she meant by "they."

A couple of weeks after the funeral, Mac informed the hospital board that he and Alexia would leave Gilead in August. He had accepted a position at a medical clinic in Camrose, Alberta, where he would be one of four doctors. There was no socialized medicine in Alberta yet, Uncle Gisli said, although that could change. Before Tommy Douglas was through, there could be socialized medicine all over the whole damned country, he said.

As we turned at the confectionery and drove down the access

road behind the cabins, I noticed how few cars were parked in the driveways. For most, the leisurely days at Whitefish Lake that summer were a memory. Soon swathing would begin. The farmers who owned most of the cabins were starting harvest, hoping to bring in their crops before the first hard frost.

I was more than ready to move back into town. I had finished swimming lessons and obtained my Advanced Intermediate badge, but after Gretchen drowned, the lake held little interest for me. Susan Mellers called on me a few times, asking if I wanted to go for a swim or an ice cream, but I always said no. I simply couldn't summon the energy friendship required. I spent most of my time reading books, going fishing with my father and mother, or walking alone in the fields where Gretchen and I had collected grasshoppers.

Sometime during those weeks, I also heard that the Krywulaks were moving to Regina, where Rosemary could get better rehabilitation for her leg. Many years later, while leafing through a health magazine in a doctor's office, I would see her picture and her title, Dr. Rosemary Krywulak-Patton, in an article about medical doctors who overcame physical disabilities. Rosemary's fifteen-year-old daughter, Alise, stood at her side, and in her daughter's eyes I detected the Rosemary I had known so long ago. Alise's eyes were those of someone who would have loved to jive.

As my mother and I drove up to our cabin that day in August, we saw that someone had left a cardboard box on the stoop. "What can that be?" said my mother. She smiled at me cheerfully, hoping, I knew, that a glint of her sunny nature would rub off on me. "I could have tried to stop them," I yearned to confide in her. But I couldn't utter those terrible words. The thought of destroying my mother's trust in her only daughter's goodness was more than I could bear. The worst part was the way she took that goodness for granted.

My mother lifted a parcel wrapped in gold foil from the box. I recognized Alexia's relaxed script on the tag.

"For Thora," she'd written. "To finish with love."

I opened the package slowly, trying not to rip the foil. That was the way I'd started to do everything in the last few weeks – slowly, hesitantly, as if by treading lightly enough through my days I wouldn't break anything, or spill anything, or create anything of value that I wouldn't be assured of keeping intact forever.

Inside was the miniature. Alexia had restored all the damage, fixed the roof and the beams and the siding, and set in new windows.

I carried the miniature out to the stoop, where I sat holding it on my knees for a long time.

Down the lake, Clement Hummel was looking for skiers.

"Why don't you go down?" my mother asked.

"I don't feel like it."

Sunday Afternoon,
JUNE 21, 1998

A picture of Markus's last days is starting to come together in my head, one that's been growing since I first came across the dampness in Markus's basement. But it's still maddeningly incomplete. I thought if I had a few more minutes alone at the Olafsson House this afternoon, before Bittner and Kramer and Longman arrived, it might help.

Through the south window of Markus's study, I view wet grass slanting in what I hope will grow into a lush hayfield. It rained this morning and the blades are still heavy with diamond drops. A few patches of blue sky break through the clouds.

From what I've read, the August day in 1914 when Markus's second eldest son was killed began a lot like this one – warm and fresh, then rainy and cool, then turning hot and sultry in later afternoon. When the thunderheads appeared, Siggi was scything in Markus's best hayfield, the one I'm looking at.

Why did he keep on scything when the storm clouds rolled

in? Why did he not run for shelter? Helga asked these questions many times in her correspondence after the accident. To my knowledge, Markus couldn't answer them. By Helga's account, he was in his study writing poetry at the time the lightning struck, and the lines he wrote that day may have been the last he produced. He hadn't been feeling well and told Helga earlier that he was going to allow himself the luxury of writing some poetry during the daylight hours.

The question is, why should his grief for Siggi, one grief among many in his life, run so deep and so long? Why could he not overcome it, he who had overcome all the hardships of homesteading and so many other deaths as well, including that of his oldest son to diphtheria?

None of the answers have come to me, but I think I'm growing closer, understanding more about Markus as I become acquainted with his physical surroundings, and begin to experience the play of light across these fields and the river.

Much planning has gone into the hayfield, which is just to the left of the family cemetery where the two eldest sons are buried. There will be a circular area of uncut grass in the centre of the field. Some interpretive guides will dress up as Markus's sons in the summer, and they'll demonstrate scything techniques for visitors. But the grass inside the circle won't be cut. Visitors will learn that the uncut grass is for the *huldufólk* – the hidden folk or "little people" who were as real to Markus's ancestors as the mountains that surrounded them. To reap a hay meadow without leaving an homage to the *huldufólk* was considered a disgrace. Worse, it could bring bad luck.

I have no direct evidence of Markus's views on any of these superstitions, although with his scientific, analytical mind, and his admiration for Darwin and the Unitarians and the American freethinkers, he almost certainly would not have believed in such spiritual manifestations as the *huldufólk,* or the ghouls, wraiths, and *afturgöngur,* or spirit walkers, that were said to haunt the graves of those who died before their time. Like Paul and Bittner and me, Markus preferred to look for truth in the evidence provided by the material world. At the same time, no doubt out of respect for many of his countrymen's beliefs, he observed such Icelandic customs as the untouched circle in the hayfield.

From the east window, I see Longman's Explorer approaching, bumping over the potholes. I replay in my mind what I told the building committee during the site selection process. "Markus chose this site, planted all the fields around it," I said. "And it was the inspiration for his life's work. Even when his neighbours fled the flooding in 1901, he stayed on."

"I will not run because others run," he wrote. "I will remain here, surrounded by the fields that I have ploughed, and the hay that I have grown, and if I leave, it will not be because danger is threatened, but because danger is real."

I step quickly into the Olafssons' kitchen, trying again to catch that picture of Markus that seems so close to revealing itself to me. Helga's cookbooks are arranged on an open whitewashed shelf: *Domestic Science and Cookery for the Young Wife; Complete Household Management; Dining and Etiquette for the Young Bride.* One of the cookbooks actually contains a recipe for blackbird pie, with real blackbirds. It gives me pleasure to imagine the kitchen bustling with Helga and her daughters making the thin pancakes called *pannecukurs* to be dotted with sugar and rolled up, ends tidily tucked under with a toothpick, until morning coffee. The thought calms me.

The fall I began reading about Markus, after the McConnells left Gilead, was also the first time I learned anything about life in Iceland. Paul, who grew up in an Anglo-Canadian home, thought this odd. Were my parents and grandparents ashamed of their past, he asked?

I had to explain that they were, if anything, intensely proud. I sometimes overheard them speaking Icelandic between themselves, and Icelandic food, *pannecukurs* and *skyr* and *hardfiskur*, were much prized and reserved for special occasions. But since we were Canadians, we would act and speak like Canadians. Not for nothing have Icelanders sometimes been called the great "blenders" in the annals of Canadian immigration. Had my parents pushed the traditions of my ancestors on me, who knows how I would have reacted? Perhaps stories of the past would have bored me.

Or could my parents have been right, after all, to try to shield me from those terrible stories – death by long starvation, volcanoes spewing cancerous air?

Towards the middle of my fourteenth summer, at my insistence, my father translated for me a portion of Markus's letters that dealt with the Icelandic idea of banishment. In those passages, Markus spoke of the tradition of forest banishment as being "one of the utmost wisdom, for what better punishment for outlawry could there be than to banish the guilty from the comradeship of their community?"

Forest banishment, he explained, was reserved for the most serious crimes – despicable acts, he called them. These could be, for instance, theft of sheep, which was considered particularly heinous, or murder of one's master. For such crimes as these, the guilty person was named an alien of society. Anyone who wished to inflict death on such an individual had the right to do so. That individual had no choice but to flee into the dark, empty wastelands of the interior.

"Such people had to hide all their lives, always in danger of being discovered and killed," Markus had written. "And yet, this was better, surely, than dying in some dungeon."

Then he posed two questions: "Is not the very knowledge of banishment useful in its own right, as a deterrent to those wild impulses that may grasp at each of us at some time during our lives, and cause us to contemplate, if only for a moment, an act that would violate the sanctity of our community? And would not the act of banishment itself hold, for the banished, the seed of purification? For while such individuals live, in such circumstances that they will do no harm to others, may they not be redeemed?"

I was too young then to know what redemption meant, but the passage deeply affected me. I would think of it as I slid into sleep; I saw myself running through deep dark forests, my feet bare, hands held out in front to sweep away the underbrush, eyes glancing back to see if anything was chasing me.

On that night in May, when I refused to let Paul look at

my girlhood photo albums, he said I was trying to banish my childhood from my life.

"That's ridiculous," I said.

"You never go back to Saskatchewan," he said. "Why is that? You said you loved growing up there, that the lakes are out of this world."

"My parents died a long time ago. You know that."

"Most people want to go back and visit the place where they grew up, at least once in a while."

"Stop hounding me."

"Stop hounding yourself, Thora."

Longman appears in the doorway, remarkably cheerful for having been called away from his Sunday afternoon oil painting sessions. Now he walks into the parlour and steps over the velvet rope. He takes his time fingering an ornate carving on a wooden chest that holds homespun blankets.

"Nice," he says.

I hear Bittner's steps coming up the stairs, quick and even. Kramer shuffles behind him.

"You better see this," Bittner says. The tightness in his voice cuts away the need for introductions. Longman and I look at each other, then follow Bittner and Kramer part way down the stairs to the basement.

The dank odour is stronger than ever. "Here," says Bittner. He taps a metal file on a portion of the concrete that's waist high. It makes a hollow sound. Then he taps along a portion of the west wall, producing a thudding sound.

"I'd say the soil has been dug out behind this wall," he says. "That's what's causing the seepage. There might have been a cistern here at one time, but I don't think so."

"So what is it?" I catch the shine of Longman's eyes even in the shadowy light of Bittner's Coleman.

"I think there's a chamber of some kind behind here," he said. "God knows why."

"What makes you think that?" I ask. Markus and Helga never wrote about any concealed chamber. They lived in more peaceful times than ours and stowed whatever few valuables they had in a small safe in Markus's study.

"I'll show you," Bittner says.

We follow him up the stairs and outside to the woodshed. Even Kramer seems interested, keeping up with me at a fast-paced clip. The earth is still soft from the rain and the air smells damp and earthy and sweet.

"Take a listen," Bittner says. He pokes the probe into the ground midway between the house and the woodshed and hands it to Longman, then to me. When I place my ear against the rubberized cup at the top of the device, I hear water running.

"Now try here," he says, placing the probe some distance from the shed. This time the sound is far away.

"I think there's a tunnel of some sort between the shed and the house," he says. "There's water running between the two, and look here." He points to the slight unevenness in the ground. "There's been some depression, which would be consistent with the existence of an underground passage."

"Where would it lead to?" I start to ask, but answer my own question. I walk over to the woodshed and unlock the door with my master set of keys. Some coal is still piled in one corner. Markus changed the heating system in the house from wood to coal early on, when miners found rich coal seams all along this part of the North Saskatchewan River Valley.

My flashlight pokes soft-edged yellow holes along the wood walls and the plank floors. Nothing. Bittner tries to push the wooden box holding the coal to the side, but it's nailed to the floor. He retrieves a crowbar from his truck and pries the box from the floor.

There it is. The pool of light circles a trap door. The boards that have been covered by the box are lighter and cleaner than the rest of the floor. How long has that box been here, I wonder? Perhaps more than eighty years. With all the other work to be done on the site, we haven't paid much attention to the woodshed. I go down on my knees and pull on the rusted latch, wondering whose hands last touched it? Could they have been Markus's?

Longman, Bittner, and Kramer crowd into the shed, but they don't say anything. I feel the weight of their anticipation on my back like a heavy wool blanket. Will this old floor hold our weight?

The door is jammed. I pull hard and it creaks open, revealing darkness. I half expect a rodent to dart out but see only blackness and then a steep ladder leading down.

"Let me have a look," Bittner says, but I'm already testing

the first rung. It's solid. Holding the flashlight in one hand, I step down into the darkness.

I descend to the last rung of the ladder and test the flooring. It's slippery, but not flooded. The air is stale and stained with wood rot. Above me, Longman and Bittner and Kramer peer down.

"Watch your step," says Bittner. He starts down himself. I waver between resentment and relief. Who knows what's down here?

The flashlight reveals a ceiling so low I can't stand straight. When I shine the light in either direction, I see a continuation of the chamber, but little else.

I start to walk faster, edging my way in front of Bittner.

"Careful," he says, but I ignore him.

And there it is, at the end of the tunnel: the wooden casket I knew would be here, the last resting place of Siggi, Markus's second eldest son. It's constructed of rough-hewn pine. Markus would have been too practical to spend money on oak or mahogany. The wood is weathered grey but otherwise in good condition. Markus set the casket on boards, a foot or so above the flooring, so even if the tunnel flooded it would probably remain intact.

I don't want to open the casket. In my haste today, I've already broken a few rules of my discipline. There's no need to disturb Siggi now, anyway. We should let him rest in peace, something Markus was never able to do.

What interests me more is the inlaid rosewood box that rests at the head of the casket. I recognize it from the old pictures I've seen of Markus's study. He kept his manuscripts in such a box.

The unlocked box easily opens. Inside, under a layer of tissue, is a sheaf of papers. Thank heavens I remembered to bring cotton gloves. I put them on and remove the tissue.

I recognize Markus's handwriting on the first page and translate for Bittner: "Sagas of the West Icelanders: An Unfinished Manuscript."

"It's the last volume of his trilogy," I tell him. "The one he'd been working on all those years."

The manuscript looks to be about eight hundred pages long, although many portions are scrawled through. I quickly riffle through them looking for a note, but there is none. That doesn't surprise me.

"At least we know now what the trouble is," Bittner says. "We should get out of here. It's probably safe enough, but it's no place to linger."

"All right." I scoop up the rosewood chest and we make our way back through the tunnel.

I climb up the ladder, relieved to be heading in the direction of air and light, and at the same time confused and ill at ease. When we reach the top and climb out, we spend a minute shaking the dirt off our faces and hands.

"So what's the conclusion?" Longman asks.

"Easy," says Bittner. "Down by the house, the tunnel's acting like a conduit for an underground stream. It's probably been there for years. It'd take river levels like we're having this spring to cause a problem."

"Fixable?" Longman again.

"Oh, yeah. It'll take a couple of days, though. I'll have to get a crew to dig into the tunnel from the outside and pour some concrete."

"But why would there be a tunnel there in the first place?" Longman asks. He looks at Bittner, then at me.

I stand with dirt still in my hair and my ears and my nostrils, and it's coming to me that I know the answer, that it's just within reach, if only I have the courage to grasp it.

"That looks like some prize," Longman says, his eyes on the manuscript.

"Yes, it is," I tell him. "I'll have it safely copied as soon as I can. Ericson and the others will be elated."

"You're not?"

"Of course I am."

Can't he see that my hands are shaking?

"But why would he leave it down there?" Longman asks. "You said there are no other known copies?"

"Who knows?" I say. "We won't really know until it's been studied."

"But you have an idea?"

"He didn't finish it," I tell him. "In fact, it looks as if he gave up on it."

"And that's why he left it down there?"

I can't answer him. Too many thoughts are swirling in my head. So much has changed that I can't yet make sense of it all.

Bittner strides over to the cellphone in his truck. Longman

follows him back to his Explorer, slapping his hands against his side pocket. There's not much for either of us to do right now. A breeze snaps up from the river and pushes me up the stoop, across the porch, into the hallway of Markus's house. The late afternoon light, caught in the rectangles of the low-slung windows, seems to emit a phosphorescent brightness. I could pull the relief I feel out of the air, wrap it, package it, tie it up with ribbons. But I still can't name it.

In ten days, the site will be crowded with visitors. They will stop to admire the placement of the Manitoba maples on the west side of the house, they will read the headstones in the family cemetery by the hayfield, they will nod in appreciation at the oak-panelled landing. Svava Erlendson will conduct tours for Icelandic guests; reporters will write features about this little-known aspect of Canadian history. The Icelandic Consul will give interviews, the Snowlands Choir will entertain. Visitors will be able to touch most of the artifacts here with their eyes, although not their hands. For at least some of them, Markus's spirit will be alive. That much I know.

When I close the door behind me in Markus's study, the voices of the visitors are stilled. Instead I hear for a moment the scratch of Markus's pen. Then the scratching stops. As it did that day in August, 1914, when his son Siggi was struck down by lightning. Struck down by lightning because Markus had asked him to work in the hayfield alone that day, so he could retreat to his study and write poetry.

Markus kept his volumes of books in glass-plated cabinets. I bend down to unlock the door of one cabinet, then straighten.

I already know what I need to know. The information was contained in those passages on folklore and superstition in *Notable West Icelanders,* the ones I gave to Carrie on Friday.

So many Icelandic customs and beliefs were bizarre, out of the Dark Ages, really, dealing as they did with the nether side of the spirit world. People about to die were said to encounter *svipurs,* or ghostlike images of themselves. Night trolls were said to haunt the countryside and freeze into stone if caught by daylight. *Huldufólk* were believed to live in rocky outcrops and be invisible to all except those with second sight. It was thought that they sometimes abducted human babies and left changelings in their place. Some inhabited lakes. Some ghouls were said to have followed their victims across the Atlantic. Many of these beliefs endured among otherwise literate Icelandic-Canadian settlers until well into the twentieth century, although Ericson has written that "it's only recently that published histories have included much information on these beliefs. Such beliefs," she wrote, "were considered unseemly among the West Icelanders, who considered themselves very rational and were most anxious to blend into mainstream Canadian society."

Bizarre as these beliefs were, surely the most grotesque concerned the *afturgöngur,* or after walkers, the spirits of the dead who were unable to rest because they had left too much unresolved in their lifetime. If the dead person died before his time, it was thought to be no easy matter to lay him to rest. The soul of such a person was believed to stay near the actual corpse until his natural lifespan had gone by, and until then the corpse would remain intact and could be troublesome.

I look out the window of the study at the hayfield, and the little family graveyard to the right. Already Bittner has placed some markers with orange tape leading nearly to the cemetery.

I don't need to examine Markus's library to recall what else I know about the *afturgöngur*. There are many records of the extreme means that Icelanders sometimes took to quiet such spirits. They would, it is said, sometimes exhume the corpse and burn it to force the spirit to leave. Sometimes they would decapitate the body and during reburial place the head under the corpse's buttocks. When such methods were employed, the hauntings in all cases are said to have stopped.

My heart is beating fast and my hands feel sweaty. So even Markus believed in ghouls, wraiths, and *afturgöngur*. Although he may only have believed in them in a metaphoric sense – surely! – they were as real to him as they were to many of his countrymen. They stalked away his sleep. They destroyed his dreams and sucked away his creativity.

It comes to me then, as perhaps I had known it would since I entered the tunnel, that none of us can be free of the *afturgöngur* in our lives unless we face them down.

A grey drizzle has started up again by the time I leave the study. The sky is clotted by wool-grey clouds. Longman is standing out on the wide veranda, his hands in his pockets.

"I think there was another reason," I tell him.

"Another reason?"

"That question you asked me, about why Markus left his

manuscript down there. I think it was because he felt guilty about his son's death."

"So why leave it down there?" Longman says, in a tone that tells me he'll have many more questions.

"I think he thought that leaving the manuscript down there was a way of atoning for Siggi's death."

"Strange," says Longman. "Siggi was killed by lightning, wasn't he? Not exactly Markus's fault."

"Markus asked him to work in the hayfield that day. He was inside, writing, when the lightning struck."

"I see," he says.

Out in the yard, the drops of rain are cold needle points on my bare legs. I walk towards the river, pushing myself against the breeze, engulfed by the rushing sound of the water and the wind teasing through the branches of the pines. We can deal with anything, I'm thinking, once we can name it. And now I have a name for what Markus suffered, and the name is guilt. Reasonable or unreasonable, they're both the same, both *afturgöngur* that will haunt you if you let them. I can see Markus now, in those final years, as I could not see him before today, defeated, blocked, drowned in guilt, digging into darkness, shovelling away in his underground tunnel, gradually working his way closer to Siggi's grave.

Or can I see anything in the past clearly? Perhaps all that is certain to me is the elemental pull of the river rushing below. Some dwarf willow to my side is half-submerged, the branches bending in and out of the current. If the river keeps up like this much longer, the roots will be sucked out of the earth and the willow join the messy flotsam of timber that bobs downstream in the current.

Perhaps the light cast the same darkening glow on that day in September, 1920, when Markus left his study and disappeared from Helga's view. I half expect to see Markus's face appearing from the water's depths, and Gretchen's, and the two of them merging and rising like wraiths, their forms soft-edged and transparent. How easy it would be to yield to this, how tempting. As Markus yielded. His words failing him when he needed them most.

And yet, when I keep my eyes fastened on the brown, churning surface of the river, no half-familiar faces appear. Dizziness comes over me, as if I could be knocked down by a slight push. My thoughts jumble and revolve. The dizziness passes, in no more time than it takes for a leaf to fall or a page to be turned. The wind drops. I'm left gathering and raking at the flotsam of those jumbled thoughts. I know now that the discontented spirit in my dreams wasn't Gretchen at all, but the faceless, restless form I have constructed to contain my guilt. No objects from the past, no records, could ever verify this belief. And yet I know unquestionably that I am right, as I know without question that the time has come for me to open that childhood photo album.

In my mind's eye, I can already see our faces in those old photographs, Gretchen's and mine, our arms over each other's shoulders, looking straight into the camera, and I know that opening that album will be far easier than keeping it closed. We'll be smiling as if nothing could ever hurt us, as if all our lives will be one shining day at the lake. Perhaps not every-thing in the picture will be exactly as I remember it. Perhaps Gretchen will be somewhat thinner. Perhaps the tilt of her chin will be just a fraction less determined. Perhaps she will be leaning on me more than I'm leaning on her, or at least just as much. Maybe we will look like sisters, as my mother said. Maybe I'll even find the seeds of forgiveness in Gretchen's eyes. Our memories and self-recriminations are wraiths, twisting and transforming and haunting our days and our nights, but only with our permission. Only if we dig them a passageway and let them through.

"Thora!"

I turn and see Paul standing in the parking lot, chatting with Longman. The noise of the river prevented me from hearing the sound of his car. He doesn't wave, just stands with his hands in his pockets, expecting me to return to my car and my life, and in his expectation I read joy and relief and respect for the space I occupy on this earth. For my halting, half-fearful footsteps across time. Although its leaves are dull and mud-splattered, the dwarf willow still holds fast to the bank.

Afterword
THE SASKATCHEWAN DOCTORS' STRIKE

The Saskatchewan doctors' strike began on July 1, 1962, when doctors were first required to bill fees exclusively through the province's new Medical Care Insurance Commission. About ninety per cent of Saskatchewan doctors closed their offices. The strike ended on July 23, 1962, following negotiations by Lord Stephen Taylor, who was brought in by the government. The two sides agreed to amendments to the Saskatchewan Medical Care Insurance Act allowing doctors the option of billing patients directly, a key point in the dispute.

As premier of Saskatchewan since 1944, T.C. Douglas led his CCF party to a majority victory in the 1960 election, with Medicare a major issue. He stepped down as premier in 1961 to assume national leadership of the newly formed New Democratic Party, and was defeated in the 1962 June federal election. The Royal Commission on Health Services, led by Mr. Justice Emmett Hall, made its final report in 1964 and recommended a national Medicare system. Within eight years, all Canadian provinces and territories agreed to participate.

Acknowledgements

A lthough *Swimming into Darkness* is a work of fiction, the author is most grateful to the following publications for providing historical background on Icelandic culture, the life and poetry of Stephan G. Stephansson, and the history of the 1962 Saskatchewan Medicare crisis:

Culture & History in Medieval Iceland. Kirsten Hastrup. Clarendon Press. Oxford, 1985.

The Icelandic Heritage. Nelson S. Gerrard. Saga Publications. Arborg, Manitoba, 1986.

Private Practice, Public Payment: Canadian Medicine and the Politics of Health Insurance 1911-1966. C. David Naylor. McGill-Queens University Press, 1986.

Stephan G. Stephansson, Selected Prose & Poetry. Translated by Kristjana Gunnars. Red Deer College Press. Red Deer; 1988.

Stephan G. Stephansson, Selected Translations from Andvökur. The Stephan G. Stephansson Homestead Restoration Committee. Edmonton, 1987.

The Icelanders in Canada. W.J. Lindal. National Publishers Ltd., and Viking Printers. Ottawa, Winnipeg, 1967.

The Icelanders of Kinmount. Don Gislason. Icelandic Canadian Club of Toronto. Toronto, 1999.

The Minister's Manual (Doran's). Edited by James W. Cox. Harper San Francisco, NY, 1992.

Unexpected Fictions: New Icelandic Canadian Writing. Edited by Kristjana Gunnars. Turnstone Press. Winnipeg, 1989.

Thanks as well to Judy Schultz for permission to use the opening quote from *Mamie's Children: Three Generations of Prairie Women,* Red Deer Press, 1997.

about the author

G ail Helgason's first book of fiction, *Fracture Patterns,* was a finalist in both the Alberta Book Awards and the City of Edmonton Book Awards. She has also had work included in a number of anthologies and literary publications. Her non-fiction books include *The First Albertans* and several travel publications.

Gail Helgason is a graduate of the University of Saskatchewan and the journalism program at Carleton University. Born and raised in Foam Lake, Saskatchewan, she lives in Edmonton.